Behind Bars

Caroline Marini

Contents

Preparing For the Club

My name is Darby Kelby and I am originally from Denver, Colorado. After graduating high school, I moved to Las Vegas, Nevada where I enrolled in college and got a basic degree in business because I didn't know what else to major in. Besides, business is something I figured would be useful for just about anything. Well, that and having some form of degree.

Now, here I am at twenty-three years old, and I have finally found and secured a job that I could actually see working out for me, one that I think I'll enjoy doing which is being a nighttime prison guard at one of the most dangerous prisons in the country, Terminus Penitentiary.

Terminus Penitentiary is home to some of America's, and possibly even the world's, most dangerous, reckless, and ruthless criminals in the world.

Yeah, I've had other jobs that I probably could have lived with - like being a bartender, for instance, since they make good pay - but I felt like I could do better than being just a bartender. So, I quit my bartending job and went searching for another job, which is why I am now a nighttime guard for Terminus Penitentiary...well, I will be in just a couple of days.

In two days, I go to Terminus Penitentiary where I will complete a one-day training. Basically, I'm walking around the Penitentiary with a higher-ranking officer, getting a feel for the place and what I'm getting myself into, but it will be during the day, even though I will be working at night. I was told it'd be during the day because they wanted me to clearly see all of the emergency exits, alarms, and whatnot, in the light for if I need them at some point during one of my shifts.

You see, hearing that probably should have freaked me the fuck out and made me turn around and say, "Thanks for the job offer but I'm going to have to pass", but honestly, it was the complete opposite for me. Hearing and knowing that just made me even more excited to work there.

What can I say? I like trouble. And then there's the fact that I know that there's a tendency for a lot of fights to break out at all hours, and I'm intrigued because that means that my work nights will be filled with excitement.

My best friend since the beginning of college, however, thinks that I'm certifiably insane for willingly wanting to work for a prison, much less going to work for one of the worst and most dangerous ones in existence.

Right now, I was getting ready to head out to some random club of my best friend, Grant's, choosing to celebrate my soon-to-be new job, and to, as he said, "enjoy your freedom and last little bit of sanity before you decide to work alongside criminals and lose both of those."

At times, he can be dramatic as hell, but hey, he's like a brother to me and I wouldn't have him any other way.

I had just finished getting out of the decently sized, all-glass shower and bathtub combination in my small, all-white, oddly modern bathroom in my apartment. The shower/bathtub wall was white with various shades of off-white textured stone, the colors matching the tiled floor while the other walls were a pristine white allowing the chrome fixtures to shine brightly when the sunlight shone in through the window in between the pedestal sink and plain toilet, the mirrored medicine cabinet placed just to the left of the window, over top of the sink.

My apartment itself is not luxurious by any means. It is rather bland with not much color or personal touches since I only have the bare necessities. It has just one bedroom and bathroom which is all I need for myself, my bedroom being the smallest thing ever with my full-sized bed squished between the walls right alongside the bathroom that was attached to my room. The main area upon entry to my apartment is really just a combination of the kitchen - which had your standard-sized appliances all squished together with a total of two storage cabinets that doubled as my pantry and utensil/kitchenware storage - and living room - an older cream couch with a couple of mismatched pillows, two random paintings hung on the wall over top of the couch, a tall plain lamp sitting on the right side of the couch, a shaggy grey rug in the center where the glass-top coffee table sat, and the forty-inch tv hung up on the opposite wall of where the couch was pressed against - with semi-worn hardwood floors throughout, all except for the bathroom of course. There was no dining area unless you count the small, grey, and white flecked laminate bar-top with three stools that I rarely used, instead opting to sit on my couch to eat while watching television. It's been my home for three years now, no matter how meager it was. Plus, it's better than living on the streets or still living at home with my parents constantly breathing down my neck about going out and making something of myself, which I am doing here in Las Vegas.

I looked through my closet which was just as small as to be expected when found in a tiny bedroom, settling on an outfit that I thought would be fine since I'm not trying to impress anyone. It consisted of a short-sleeved plaid button-up and a simple pair of dark blue jeans with plain white sneakers, nothing too special but also nothing that made me look like a mess.

I grabbed my house keys and phone before exiting my apartment, heading downstairs to wait on the Uber that I had called before getting in the shower, only waiting about five minutes until it pulled up. I climbed in, telling them the club name as I settled into my seat for the short ride.

We arrived relatively quickly so I paid the driver and got out, walking up toward the club where I immediately caught sight of Grant standing near the front doors, nodding and grinning at me the moment he spotted me.

"Wasn't sure if you were coming," he said as he pulled me in for a brief hug, slapping my back as he did so.

"Why wouldn't I? You said you'd pay for my drinks," I smirked making him scowl.

"I knew I shouldn't have said a damn thing about that," he grumbled, more to himself than me yet I still heard him clearly.

"Yeah, but you did, now come on. I want to get shit-faced."

"You never get shit-faced, though," he pointed out.

"Yeah, because I'm normally the one paying for my own drinks. But tonight you've got the tab," I said as I slapped my hand against his back like he did to mine earlier, making him groan.

"I'm so going to go broke tonight," he grumbled as we entered the club together and headed straight to the bar, ordering our first round.

The first of many more rounds that I plan on having tonight.

A Quick Fix

I didn't hesitate to quickly throw back my first drink, signaling for another immediately after. After I'd thrown back my second drink, I turned to face Grant who was pouting like a kid.

"Come on, let's go find some girls. It's going to be a while before I get my dick wet again so I plan on finding someone tonight and you should too," I nudged his arm with a grin.

"Yeah, it might make me feel a little better about the big dent in my bank account that I'll see tomorrow morning after you drink all my money away tonight," he huffed out.

"Let's just go find some chicks," I chuckled, ignoring his dramatics.

He finished his drink and set his glass down, giving me a nod before he followed me out to the dance floor, my eyes scanning the dance floor as I looked for a good fuck for tonight.

"Shit, I've found my girl. I'm out," Grant said making me chuckle as he made a B-line through the large crowd with his sight set on a fake blonde, his preferred type of girl. I, on the other hand, wasn't a fan of blondes. I liked the dark-haired ones and only the dark-haired ones.

I let my own eyes roam over the vast sea of people, stopping when my eyes landed on a girl in a dark corner of the club. Her dark eyes were already locked on my frame as she scanned me from head to toe, not making eye contact with me just yet. When she finally noticed that I was looking at her, she gave me a seductive smile and slowly beckoned me over by crooking her index finger at me as she leaned languidly back against the wall. I smirked back at her, not hesitating to make my way through the crowd, and walked straight up to her. I didn't waste any time as I pressed her back even further against the wall, locking my lips against hers and not giving her a chance to speak or even move. It didn't matter anyway since she instantly crumbled against me, letting me take complete control of her, more than willingly.

I pulled back from her lips, placing kisses down her neck and throat, listening to the contented moans that slipped passed her lips, urging me to press my growing erection against her, grunting at the straining of it against the inside of my jeans.

"I don't care how big of a douche I'm about to sound like but fuck it. I don't want to know your name and I don't want to hear your voice. All I want is to have a nice quick fuck, which seems like you're only interested in, too. So what's going to happen is I'm going to fuck you right here, right now. Moan if you understand," I said, giving a pleased smirk at the soft moan she let out in response. "Perfect. I'm going to fuck you now."

I unzipped and unbuttoned my pants, pulling them down and my boxers down. I didn't push either of them very far down my legs, only wanting just a bit of room to pull my cock out to fuck her. I reached into my back, right pants pocket, and pulled out the condom that I kept in most of my pants just in case the urge struck, or I found a hot girl to fuck. I ripped it open before sliding the tight rubber quickly down my cock. Once my cock was wrapped up, I reached up under her black leather mini-skirt and pushed her soaked thong to the side, quickly thrusting inside with haste.

The moment my cock was inside her, it felt like I was just in a vast open space. She was so fucking loose that it wasn't even any good. Honestly, it was awful but I needed to get my release since it would be only God knows how long until the next opportunity presented itself. So, regardless of how unsatisfying the feeling was, I began to thrust upward, focused on her huge, barely-covered tits as I chased my orgasm. It felt like just a few seconds had passed before she was crying out her release, her body being wracked by a shiver.

Finally, after what felt like forever, I came in the condom which I quickly pulled off and tossed into a nearby trashcan. Funnily enough, I'm pretty sure it was filled with other used condoms that were practically spilling all over the floor surrounding it.

I pulled up my boxers and pants, zipping them up quickly so that I could get the fuck out of there as soon as I possibly could. I at least had the decency to look at the girl again, shooting her a wink and a smirk.

"Thanks. Have a nice night."

Then I was turning around and practically sprinting over to the bar where I ordered a nice, strong spiced rum, downing it as soon as it was placed in front of me, waving for another one the second it was gone. Once I was given that one, I downed it, too, enjoying the slight burn that tingled the inside of my throat.

I felt a few hard slaps on my right shoulder, prompting me to look to my left to see Grant with a broad smile on his face, looking relaxed and happy as hell. It seemed like he had lucked out and gotten a good fuck, the lucky bastard.

"Hey! How was the fuck? I saw you and some girl in the corner!" He grinned making a grimace instantly contort my features.

"Please don't remind me. She was so fucking loose that I wasn't sure if I would cum or not, so I focused on her big ass tits, and then came after staring at them for like thirty minutes."

He busted out laughing, obviously enjoying my pain and suffering.

"Oh, that's fucking great!" He cackled, wiping away imaginary tears.

"Glad you enjoyed yourself," I said with a roll of my eyes.

"Oh, I definitely did. Too bad you didn't," he sniggered making me roll my eyes as I finished my third spiced rum.

"Look, tonight's been a bust so I'm just going to head home," I said as I set my now empty glass onto the bar top before lifting a hand to run through my already tousled hair.

"Already?!" He exclaimed, looking at me in disbelief.

"Yeah, I feel like I should sterilize my cock even though I was wrapped," I shuddered in disgust, remembering the awful feeling.

He laughed again and nodded.

"Okay. Text me when you can."

"I will. Night," I said, giving him one last quick hug and pat on the back.

I turned around and left the club, hopping into a cab that had just let out a few people, and heading home. Once home, I stripped, showered thoroughly, and then pulled on some clean boxers before collapsing tiredly in bed, falling fast asleep within seconds.

Terminus Penitentiary Tour

It's been two days since my shitty fuck and, honestly, I would have been better off going home with a case of blue balls. At least then I wouldn't feel more pent up now than I did before I went. But, pushing that thought aside, I focused on my current task of heading to the Penitentiary for my guided, daytime tour.

I pulled up to the front gate where a bored-looking guard was standing in the guard shack wearing what looked like a stereotypical security guard uniform: a long-sleeved light blue button-down shirt, navy tie, black slacks, and most likely polished black shoes or something similar, but I couldn't see his feet. It was odd to me since this is a prison after all, and not some mall or movie set.

"What can I help you with?" He asked, his tone matching his expression.

"I'm here to meet up with Sergeant Barrin Bishop for a tour of the Penitentiary," I explained to the guard. There was no use in trying to sound upbeat or overly excited, especially with how little the guard seemed to care. Hell, he seemed pretty irked by my presence, even though he had probably been sitting doing nothing for who knows how long before I showed up.

"Okay. What's your name?" He asked, his voice monotone.

"Darby Kelby."

"Can I get some identification to prove that you are who you say you are?" He asked, seemingly getting more annoyed the longer I sat there and interacted with him, even with our limited interaction.

"Oh! Yeah sure, here you are," I said reaching into the cupholder beside me where my wallet sat, my ID tucked inside which I pulled out for him. I handed it over, and he gave it a quick scan before nodding and grabbing his walkie-talkie off of the small table in front of him. He spoke quickly into it, pausing to hear whatever he was told in response. It was kind of staticky sounding on the other end, so I couldn't understand a thing, but he ended up handing me my ID back.

"Go ahead. Park in the lot to your left, in one of the first two rows. After that, head up to the door and enter the office. Once in there, Sergeant Bishop will be waiting for you," he said, giving a brusque wave in the general direction he had just told me to go to.

"Alright, thanks," I said with a nod in acknowledgment before driving off. There was no use in doing anything else since he obviously wanted me gone.

I followed his instructions, parking in one of the rows he told me to before exiting my car and locking it as I walked up to the office, and opening the door. Upon walking inside, I saw a large, rather buff guy standing waiting with his arms crossed loosely over his chest muscled chest that looked on the brink of bursting the buttons to his slate gray, long-sleeved button-up shirt. He had his brown hair styled up and out of his face with a slight curl to it, a light, full beard covering his jaw, just over his upper lip, and under his bottom lip as well, the hair there a similar medium brown color to the hair on his head. His eyes were an icy blue color that seemed to pierce into my soul as I approached him, causing me to straighten my posture up ever so slightly.

"Darby Kelby?" He asked me, his face stoic and emotionless as his eyes slowly moved over me, analyzing me.

"Yes, sir, that's me. Which makes you Sergeant Barrin Bishop?" I guessed, making sure to sound as respectful as I could.

He suddenly smiled wide which I wasn't expecting, nor the hand that he extended out to me to shake.

"Yes, I am. You can call me Sarge or Bishop, I don't mind either of them," he said with almost more enthusiasm than a high school cheerleader.

"Yes sir," I said with a slight smile, taking his outstretched hand and giving it a firm shake that he returned with one of his own.

"Cut the 'sir' shit. I know I'm old but I don't want to be reminded of it," he said with a slight shake of his head.

"Oh, okay, si- I mean, Bishop," I said, catching myself at the last second.

He smiled and chuckled at me in response which had me letting out my own little laugh.

"Now, why don't you just follow me so we can begin your tour?" He asked, extending his arm forward for me in an overdramatic fashion.

"Alright," I agreed as I proceeded forward with him at my side, though I let him go a little ahead of me since I didn't know where we were headed.

"So, we're going to start here in the office for a bit. There are a few more documents that you need to sign, and then we'll continue on," he said.

I nodded as he led me into a nearby office where there were a few documents that I signed about my health insurance, my social security number, and a personal as well as emergency contact form which I signed after looking over them.

"Here you go," I said after standing up, handing the completed papers over to him.

"Thank you. Let me just quickly file these away, and then we can continue on," he said with a grin as he placed them in a large, nearby filing cabinet, turning back to me afterward. "And done. Okay, let's go."

He then led me back out of the office that we were in, down the hallway, turning to the left where we exited a set of doors. We walked back outside in between two, at least, twenty-foot fences on either side of us. One side was completely covered in rings upon rings of shining, sharp barbed wire that was used to keep the prisoners from escaping, while the other side was similar to that of the walls and bars of a standard jail cell you'd see on TV. I had no doubt that both sides of the fencing were also electrified for an added security measure.

"Okay, so this is the way you go to get from the main office and parking lot, all the way to the back to the section where you will be working," Bishop explained.

"Okay, so every time I come here, I just go this way?" I asked for extra clarification.

"Yes, that is correct. Now up here, around this turn, is the section you're working in."

We turned the corner and then took a momentary pause at another set of gates where he swiped his ID over the reader. The gates unlocked and we walked in after Bishop ensured that the gates had fully locked behind us once more. After that, we walked about fifty more yards to the actual building I'd be working in where there was another reader that he swiped his card on before we actually entered the main building, and cell block that I would be working in.

The inside looked like a public school cafeteria with all the solid, metal hexagonal tables with attached round metal seats that were bolted into the ugly, green laminated tile floors. It was a rather wide open space that consisted of the same ugly green color for the metal stairs and guard rails leading up to the second floor of the building. The sides of the room were occupied by beige, solid metal doors with a singular, skinny rectangular window that looked into each of the prisoner's cells for the convenience of the guards. The only wall that didn't contain cells was the one at the very front where you entered, but there was also a large, secured room directly to the right of the main door upon entry where I could see some guards milling about inside. There was also an area near the front, but off to the side where there were eight phones, all of which were being used by the inmates, long lines forming behind them as others waited for their turn to use the phone.

The first thing that I noticed after looking around at what was in the building was that it was pretty damn full of prisoners who were just sitting around at different tables in sections and groups. Some were glaring at each other, others glaring at the guards stationed along the walls and in the secured room, and then there were a few mixed in who looked absolutely petrified, none of which included those standing in line for the phones.

As I looked at the petrified ones that were scattered throughout, I couldn't keep from thinking that they did this shit to themselves. They fucked up big time, so they had to face the consequences of their actions, so they had no reason to be scared. They should have thought more before doing whatever it was they did to wind up here, and maybe then they wouldn't be practically shitting themselves now.

I followed Bishop to a large door that lead into the secured guards' room that I had noticed earlier. The door looked to be made of reinforced steel, just proving to me how secure it was as he, again, used his ID to scan on the reader before pulling the obviously heavy door open. He walked inside with me walking right behind him as we entered what was obviously a room meant solely for the guards and their protection as I had originally surmised from first glance. There were quite a few guards in here, some just sitting down and watching camera feeds of prisoners all throughout the building while others were at the lockers behind it, obviously getting ready for a shift change.

"So these are two guards that actually normally work the night shift but came in to help out the day shift today," Bishop said, leading me over to two men at neighboring lockers. "The one on the left is Ryan Robledo, and on the right is Patrick Ernst. Ryan, Patrick, this is Darby Kelby. He is the new night guard we hired," Bishop introduced us.

"Fucking finally! We've been dying for another guard to help out at night when these dickheads decide to be stupid!" The one he'd said was Patrick exclaimed in relief. Patrick had dark, honey-brown curly hair with heavy stubble and dark blue, almost appearing black, eyes.

"No offense, but aren't you a kid?" The other named Ryan asked me, looking me over with amusement. Ryan, on the other hand, was clearly a slightly older man with salt and pepper brown hair with matching lightly stumbled beard, and a set of blue-grey eyes.

What the fuck was up with these guys all looking similar?! Did they have to hire me for some kind of demographic change or something?

I gave him a hard, cold stare in response to his question. I hated being called a kid, even when I was one because it always resulted in people treating me as though I couldn't do a damn thing for myself which pissed me the fuck off.

"I'm twenty-three years old," I said.

"So you are a youngster," Ryan nodded to himself, grinning ever so slightly.

"Yeah? Well, at least I'm out trying to make a living instead of sitting on my ass or getting drunk somewhere like other kids my age, right?" I fired back, trying to keep my temper in check but unable to bite back the comment.

That's all I need to do: let my temper get the best of me and wind up getting fired before I even start. Hell, not like it'd be the first time it's happened, and I can guarantee that it wouldn't be my last time, either.

Both the guards grinned at each other and nodded before turning back to face Bishop and me.

"The kid's got balls, I'll give him that," Ryan said, now chuckling.

"Yeah, and there's no doubt that he'll be just fine," Patrick added with an appreciatory nod.

Wait...Were they trying to test me?

Based on the smiles they're giving me right now, I'm going to go with a yes, and it seems like I passed. I guess I did something right so far, I just have to keep it up. Intentional or not.

"Alright, well Darby, this is pretty much everything for now. When you get here for your first day, I'll be waiting in the front office for you so we can get you your identification badge to be able to move about the Penitentiary freely, got it?" Bishop said.

"Yeah, sounds good," I nodded.

"Alright then. I'll walk you out," Bishop said.

With that, I nodded at Ryan and Patrick who gave me nods back in return, before following Bishop back up to the front office. Once there, I thanked him for the tour, collected my uniform, and then headed back home to start my new, adjusted sleep schedule that I would now have for however long I lasted at Terminus Penitentiary.

A Storm's A Brewing

The day has finally come, though, I guess it could be considered night, too. Regardless, it's my first shift tonight and I'm so damn pumped. I can't wait to start and truly get the feel of my new workplace.

I had just changed into my uniform that I had gotten before leaving yesterday which was a slate-grey long-sleeved shirt with the same, matching colored long pants, a black leather belt with a plain silver buckle threaded through the loops of my pants, and I had bought myself a nice pair of black work boots a few days after being notified I had gotten the job, way before yesterday's facility tour. I, honestly, was just happy I didn't have the same stereotypical security uniform as the bored guard in the front parking lot did.

Before leaving my apartment, I grabbed a granola bar and a bottle of water to take with me for something to snack on and stay hydrated. After making sure I had everything I needed, I headed off to the Penitentiary. The drive seemed to pass by in the blink of an eye, taking me hardly any time to arrive this time around because of the fact that I was so focused on making sure I got there a little early so I could get done with everything necessary before officially starting my first shift.

When I pulled up the guard shack, the same front gate guard was still there and still looking just as bored in the same uniform. Before I could even speak, he started to talk, not even allowing me to get a single sound out.

"You're the new night guard, I know. We talked yesterday and I was told ahead of time. Go ahead inside and park wherever."

"Alright, thanks," I said as I drove in and parked in the spot in the dead center of the lot, grabbing my phone, wallet, keys, water bottle, and granola bar before getting out of my car, locking it behind me as I walked to the office. Just as I walked in, Bishop came walking from the back of the office, a few file folders in his hands.

"Oh, Darby! You're here early," he chuckled, having not expected me to be almost a half-hour early. What can I say, I wanted to make a good impression since I had a good feeling about this place.

"Yeah, I figured I'd get here early so I could get everything done and sorted before I headed back to my unit," I told him with a slight nod in greeting.

"Damn, I wish some of the other guys got here early like you. Would make shit a lot easier," he said with a wistful sigh that just had me nodding my head. I didn't know what to say in response, so I figured that would be a safe thing to do.

"If you're busy right now, I don't mind waiting," I said, not wanting to bother him with my early appearance.

"No, I'm not busy. In fact, these files need to go in the same direction where we need to go to get your identification card, so just follow me," he said with a nod that signaled me to follow after him, which I did. He led me into a medium-sized, plain white room with a camera set up on a tripod. "Just give me a quick second to run these files just a few doors down, and when I come back we'll snap a quick picture and get it printed out on your card for you."

"Go ahead, you're good," I told him, stepping to the side to allow him to pass by me.

He nodded his head and then ran back out with the files, coming back maybe five minutes later if that. My picture was quickly taken and then I was told to have a seat off to the corner in the same room I had gotten my picture taken while he went to go print my badge, card, whatever you want to call it, in a separate room. He was gone about fifteen minutes before returning, handing me my Terminus Penitentiary badge.

"I'm going to walk back with you. There's been talk of a possible brawl occurring tonight so I want to be there in case it actually happens," Bishop explained.

"Alright. Sounds like my first night is going to be interesting already," I said as I gave a half-smile while he chuckled.

"You work for Terminus Penitentiary now. Every night you're here is going to be interesting," he said, flashing me yet another bright grin.

"Well, at least I know that I won't be bored," I said with a shrug.

"Here, you never will be, and that's a promise," he said, an odd look briefly flicking through his eyes.

He scanned his badge and we walked through the large gates, closing them behind us, before continuing down the walkway and into the unit I would be spending my nights in for the foreseeable future.

As we walked in, some other guards nodded to me as they walked out, looking tired as hell but not like the stereotypical asshole prison guards that you always hear about.

"Darby, why don't you head on over to the guard's room in the back and pick one of the empty lockers to put your things in? I'll be back there in a bit to come to get you," Bishop said, his eyes scanning the unit for something or someone.

"Alright, see you in a bit then," I said as I walked to the door and scanned my badge just like I had seen Bishop do, opening the large door once the reader turned green, and walking inside after shutting the door behind me.

"Hey, Darby," Patrick said, looking up to grin at me from where he was sitting in a chair that was parked in front of the series of monitors that showed live footage of the prisoners in the other room.

"Hello," I greeted, nodding back at him while keeping my face straight as I went over to the empty locker on the far end of the wall, putting my few things inside of my chosen locker.

"Do you ever smile, kid?" Ryan asked with a chuckle who was sitting in an adjacent chair to Patrick's also facing the monitors.

I pushed my annoyance back at the nickname, realizing that I was probably going to be stuck with it since I was the youngest one here.

I shrugged my shoulders before turning from my locker and heading back over to stand in between, yet slightly behind, both Patrick and Ryan's desk chairs. Their eyes flitted between me and the monitors, yet the grins they wore never faded. It was kind of creepy how much these guards smiled what with where they worked and all, especially in comparison to the security guard out in the guard shack.

"On occasion," I shrugged.

"What kind of occasion?" Ryan pressed, brow raised curiously.

"When I'm with people I actually know," I responded, finding no reason to lie.

"You're going to be a tough nut to crack, and you know what? Challenge accepted," Patrick grinned at me making me frown slightly in confusion. Yeah, they were really fucking creepy, and weird too.

"Challenge? What challenge?" I asked, looking between the two men.

"It's the challenge to make you treat us like friends. We'll end up being friends anyways, though, since we're going to be here pretty much every night together, but I want to see just how quickly I can soften you up," Patrick grinned at me crookedly.

"Um, okay, if that's what you want to do, go ahead," I said as I stared directly at him with a brow raised while he continued to grin at me. I didn't see his challenge working out so well for him, but hey, whatever floats his boat. If he wanted to try, who was I to stop him? Plus, I was interested in seeing what he had in store.

Our little stare-off lasted about five more minutes when I heard the door open, prompting him to turn away first, so I did the same, turning my head to see Bishop coming in looking a mix of both pissed and worried.

"What's up, Bishop?" Ryan asked, instantly on alert upon seeing our superior's expression.

"There's definitely going to be a damn riot here tonight," Bishop growled, reaching a hand up to rub irritatedly at his face.

"Why? What's happening that is making you think that there's definitely going to be one?" Patrick questioned next, leaning forward some in his chair.

"The fucking Nordics and Italians are at each other's throats even more so now than they were before. It's no longer just the members, it's the fucking heads now too," Bishop growled once more.

"Fuck!" Ryan and Patrick cursed, looking a bit panicked now too.

I didn't have a clue as to what they were talking about, but I had enough sense to know that whatever they were talking about must be really bad. But, I needed to ask to know what exactly I would soon enough be in for.

"I'm lost. Would someone fill me in on what's going on?" I asked.

"Shit, sorry Darby. I forgot that you don't know all about the Mafias and shit yet," Bishop sighed, scrubbing at his face even more, evidently a nervous or stressed tick of his.

Both of my brows rose in shock at what he had just said.

"Mafias? Those are still around?"

"Yeah, and they're so much worse now than they ever were back in the 1920s and shit!" Ryan growled, standing up and beginning to pace around the office space.

"So there are Mafia members locked up in here?" I asked, wanting to get as much information as I could while we had a bit of time.

"Yeah, and so are both Mafia leaders. Those two always cause a fuck ton of problems for us, and everyone else in the Penitentiary, not just this unit. They despise each other and are always trying to kill each other and anyone else who tries to get in between them," Patrick said, glaring at nothing in particular.

I was getting ready to ask another question about the two leaders and who they were so I knew who to look out for when a loud, screeching alarm began to go off all around the unit, the sound echoing around inside the office. Patrick leaped to his feet from the chair while both Bishop and Ryan tensed up.

"Fuck! It looks like they've already started!" Bishop yelled angrily before turning to face me. "Darby, I know it's your first night, but I need you to prepare for battle. These guys are major criminals, and when they start fighting, they go after everyone who isn't a part of their Mafia. All their interested in is death and blood."

I nodded my head at him in understanding as a slight chuckle escaped my lips that had quirked up into a smirk at his words that had a thrum of excitement shooting down my spine.

"Don't worry about me, Bishop. I can handle my own," I told him.

"Good. Now let's go handle these guys," he said. Then our group of four were marching for the door that led out into the fray.

Going into Battle

C haos.

That's what I would use to describe everything I was seeing in front of me right now.

Complete, and utter, chaos.

The moment we stepped out of the door, exiting the guard's area, there were piles upon piles of guys on top of each other everywhere as they exchanged blows with one another. I could see some other guards also mixed in the piles, trying to pull them apart, but most were getting sucked right into them.

Seeing all of the fights and hearing the yelling, cussing, and screaming set my blood on fire as the adrenaline kicked in all throughout my body, instantly preparing me to 'go into battle', as Bishop had said.

"Darby, go over to those guys on the right and pull them apart! The Tact Teams are almost here to help keep them separated!" Bishop instructed.

"What about you, Sarge?" Patrick asked, seeming worried.

"I need to look for the two assholes who started all this shit in the first place!" Bishop growled out, getting angrier and angrier as time wore on and the fights turned more brutal around us.

With that, we all split up to go and do our part in attempting to end this shitshow. I ran over to the two closest guys to me who were exchanging blow after blow with each other. I grabbed them each by the collars of their standard, tan Penitentiary prison outfits and jerked them apart before slamming them against the wall they had been fighting against while simultaneously pushing them away from each other as they screamed obscenities at each other and me, not fazing me in the slightest.

"Yeah, whatever. You two are the dumbasses who got yourselves into this mess," I said as I twisted each of their arms tightly. It wasn't enough to break them but enough for it to hurt and show them that I wasn't going to take their shit.

They stopped struggling but kept on yelling and cussing. I ignored it though, looking up to see the Tact Team rushing in, made apparent based on the fact that they looked like S.W.A.T. guys since they wore thick black gear with the words TACT TEAM printed in white across the chest of their thick vests. Two guys rushed over to me, taking the two idiots I had and hauling them off to deal with them, keeping them separated, while I turned to go and help pry more guys apart.

I saw Ryan in the middle of four guys who were trying to go after each other. He had a split lip, and a busted nose from what I could tell based on the blood steadily dripping from it, making me rush over to help him out.

I grabbed two of the guys who seemed to be on the same side as they each tried to choke one of the other guys. I didn't hesitate to pin them to the wall, the same as I had done with the first two dumbasses. I saw the guy in my right hand kick his leg out to try and leg sweep me, but I was quick to slide back, taking my own right leg and wrapping it around his feet, jerking my leg back and sending him crashing down to the ground on his knees. I wasted no time in turning and doing the same to the other guy, not wanting him to try and get the upper hand on me, though I doubted he would.

"Shit, kid! Where'd you learn to do that?" Ryan questioned after having subdued the other two to the best of his ability. He looked at me in awe making me uncomfortable by how closely he seemed to be looking at me, as though he could figure out how I had taken down the two men that were almost bigger than I was.

"My dad taught me," I said, the words coming out stiffly.

"Damn! You were fast, too! Thanks for the help!" Ryan said, seeming to snap from his trance.

"No problem, that's what I'm here for," I said, wanting to end the conversation there.

It thankfully did when a few Tact guys came running over, grabbing the inmates from us and latching cuffs around their wrists.

"Okay, let's see who else needs help," Ryan said, looking at me as he wiped some of the endless streams of blood away from his mouth with the back of his hand, only serving to smear it across his face. It didn't matter anyway because more was dripping down his face the entire time.

"Yeah," I agreed as I looked around to see who else needed help.

Suddenly, a loud yell broke through the shouts of everything else.

"AHH! MOTHER FUCKER!"

"That's Bishop!" Ryan cried out, having easily detected who the loud cry of pain had come from.

Hearing that my superior was most likely in trouble, and definitely in some sort of pain, had me sprinting off in the direction the cry had come from.

I pushed past the many Tact Team guys, looking left and right for any sign of where Bishop might possibly be. I could hear both Ryan and Patrick, who had hurried over at the familiar voice's cry, right behind me as I shoved through the other inmates, guards, and Tact Team members. I rounded a corner at the very far end of the room, my steps faltering momentarily at the sight before me which had my blood boiling in my veins.

Bishop was attempting to separate two big, burly guys wrestling around on the ground, throwing punches that put all the others I had seen previously to shame, yet neither man appeared to be too fazed by any of them. The light from above glinted on something small that was embedded in Bishop's bicep, sticking out some and allowing me to easily identify what it was and wha had happened.

The bastards had stabbed him.

I charged at the two fighting men, grabbing the one on top of the pile. He was blonde and much bigger than the other dark-haired guy he was fighting, but the dark-haired guy wasn't too much smaller. I was quick to slam him roughly against the wall, using the same tactic as before, yet he managed to free one of his hands from my hold and swing his fist at my face, connecting with my jaw in one solid, swift punch. It probably hurt like hell but I was currently too pissed and full of adrenaline to feel any pain. It didn't mean that I didn't want, oh so badly, to beat the fuck out of him though. Because, fuck, did I.

Instead of trying to nail him in the face myself in retaliation, I quickly swept his legs out from under him when he wasn't expecting it, using another one of my previous tricks. He dropped down to the ground hard, his eyes wide with shock as he looked up at me before a nasty glare quickly contorted his features, and he began growling and snarling angrily at me.

"You just fucked up!" He roared, his voice deep and rough from the force behind his words. I could also vaguely detect some sort of European accent, but I didn't pay too much mind to it.

"Keep quiet," I shot back, waiting for the Tact Team to come and collect him from me as I kept him grounded.

Ryan was checking on Bishop's stab wound while Patrick kept the other guy pressed to the ground with his hands pinned against his back, holding them together as he kneeled beside him, preventing any movement from him. Not even so much as a wiggle.

"Who the fuck even are you?!" The guy I was holding down snarled at me, still trying to fight me off.

"Doesn't matter. You don't need to know," I said emotionlessly, not wanting to have to interact with this guy more than necessary.

Just then, the Tact Team finally came, hauling off both the inmates while a doctor from the Penitentiary who had come to check on and attend to the injured inmates, tended to Bishop's stab wound.

As all that was occurring, I was leaned against one of the walls, arms crossed over my chest as I quietly watched everything happen.

"Darby, come here for a minute," Bishop called me over from where he was sat on a chair that someone had brought for him to sit on while the stitches had been sewn.

I walked over to him, staying a little back to keep out of the doctor's way as they finished stitching up his arm from the knife wound. Lucky for him, it wasn't too bad but it did need a couple of stitches that would take no time to heal, the threading dissolving once he was fully healed according to what I had heard the doctor say to him as they cleaned up and repacked all of the used and unused materials.

"Yeah, Bishop?" I questioned.

"I want to thank you for the help with those two," he said with a nod of appreciation.

"It was nothing. I couldn't let you-" I started to shake off his thanks, only for him to interrupt me.

"But you may want to keep an eye out for Calder," he said, sounding more serious than I had ever heard him thus far.

"Who's Calder?" I asked, unable to stop the furrow in my brow from the confusion of who he was talking about.

"He's the bug blonde guy you took down just a few minutes ago. No one has ever taken him down before," Patrick said, joining the conversation, looking at me worriedly.

"Oh, him? That was nothing," I said with a shrug. For me, it really was. He wasn't paying enough attention to my movements, so it was easy to capitalize of his distractedness.

"Yeah, well, anyway, he's pissed and even though today's only your first day, I like you, Darby. You stepped up and showed that you aren't going to let these guys walk all over you. I'd hate for something to happen to you because of that bravery and confidence though," Bishop said, concern edging into his voice. Concern that I didn't want him to have about me.

"Don't worry about me, Bishop. I can handle myself," I said, brushing him off. I wasn't too concerned, even if he was dangerous. I am a big boy and could deal with whatever was thrown my way, it wouldn't be the first time I had to watch out for trouble.

"Yes, but you don't have to with us here. We want to help you," Bishop insisted.

"I appreciate it, but I think I'll be okay," I said as I nodded at them and then walked back down the hallway, into the destroyed main area that doubled as the dining area of the unit. There was food, drinks, decks of cards, and other junk littered everywhere as well as several places where there were either drops or small puddles of blood. I think I even saw a few teeth on the ground, too.

Clean-up is going to be a bitch.

His Return

ONE WEEK LATER

It's been a week since my first day at the Penitentiary, which also included dealing with my first riot.

For now, everything is fine except for the few glares and stares that I get from some of the inmates who, as Patrick and Ryan told me, are a part of the Nordic Mafia. They said that they are trying to figure me out and who I am after having taken down their boss without difficulty.

They can try all they want, but I'm not saying anything to anyone about my personal life because it is just that: my personal life. They don't need to know that, and they won't. I am here to do my job, which is watching these criminals like some kind of babysitter.

Ever since the riot broke out, the blonde guy, Calder as I was told his name was, has been locked up in isolation for the week as punishment for his part in the riot, but tonight he gets let out back into the main unit with the other inmates. The other guy, whose name I learned is Enzo, won't be out for at least another week since the security camera footage caught him being the one who stabbed Bishop in the bicep, not only that but he was said to have thrown the first punch which had started it all, hence why his punishment was longer. Bishop was fine, never letting the minor injury slow him down. If anything, I think he was doing more than was necessary, all in an effort to prove that he was perfectly fine. He said it was nothing but a scratch, and that he had dealt with way worse. Working here and seeing my first riot, I found that easy to believe.

Patrick, Ryan, and Bishop have all said that they've got my back if Calder decides he wants to try anything, but to be honest, I'm not worried by him in the slightest. I've known guys like him, they're all bark and no bite. Besides, even if he does bite, he'll just get sent back to isolation for a few days, and it will be no one's fault but his own. And, as I've said many times before, I can take care of myself.

I was also still sporting a semi-bruised jaw thanks to that punch he threw. I was right when I had said I would feel it later after my adrenaline wore off, and fuck, did I. I felt it the next day when I woke up and could barely open my mouth at first, my jaw was so damn sore. But now it's fine aside from the discoloration and slight ache every now and then, and even that didn't bother me.

Currently, I was standing with my back pressed against one of the walls on the side of the unit near the cells, all of which were open for the inmates to come and go. I was watching the inmates, scanning for any possible trouble when I heard the sound of the doors that led to the back of the building where the isolation cells in the unit were located, opening up with a beep as the automatic locks were disengaged followed by the beep again as they were re-engaged upon closing.

A moment later, in walked the man known as Calder. Now that he wasn't trying to attack me or anyone else, I took the time to look over him. He was about six foot five in height, though probably more since I could only see him from a distance. His hair was a pale blonde color that seemed to shine when the overhead, cheap fluorescent lights hit it, and a set of dark, blue-green eyes that resembled an ocean right before a hurricane was set to pass through. His bared biceps and arms which were visible from the short-sleeved prison uniform shirt were covered in tattoos that seemed to seamlessly bleed together. All in all, he was truly a monster of a man if his fighting skills didn't previously show it.

He was flanked by four guards which I found unbelievable seeing as how I was at least half his size, maybe even less, and I managed to take him down with no problem. Maybe these guards needed some harder training.

He looked at a table that had two, slightly larger guys sitting at it, though both were visibly smaller than him. I watched as the two guys nodded in my direction when they looked at him, causing the blonde guy to turn to face me, a smirk on his face as he began to make his way over to me.

Great. Time to deal with him and whatever bullshit he plans on saying or doing.

I watched with a blank face as he got closer and closer to me until he was about four, maybe five feet away from me, and he stopped, staring at me with that smirk still on his face.

"So, Darby, I heard you're the new guy," he finally spoke.

Not sure how he knew my name after being locked up in isolation, but I didn't really care either as I continued to stare at him wordlessly with the same blank look on my face. My silence seemed to strike a chord in him and piss him off.

"Answer me when I speak to you!" He shouted at me, swinging his fist forward and punching the wall a few inches from the right side of my head. I didn't even flinch as I continued to stare at him. I was incredibly amused at how easily I seemed to piss him off by doing and saying nothing.

I watched his eyes to see that he was both surprised and impressed at my nonreaction, but the emotions were only there for a split second before they were replaced, yet again, with anger. It must be his expression and emotion of choice.

"Are you fucking stupid?! Do you have a death wish?!" He screamed at me again, but just like I have been, I continued to stare blankly at him and remain silent.

"Why you stupid little mother fuc-" He went to yell at me, again, when Bishop came hurrying over and cut him off.

"Do we have a problem over here guys?" Bishop asked as he looked in between us, eyes lingering on me for a moment, looking at me as if I had lost my mind.

Bishop had opted to change shifts from the daytime to the nighttime since he said he wanted to make sure they stayed in line before they get shut in for the night for bed, but I think it's actually because he wanted to watch over me in case one of the Nordic Mafia members targeted me.

As if I needed his or anybody else's protection.

Just to piss off Blondie, I spoke to Bishop, turning my bored stare away to look at my superior, and then I purposely said his name wrong, because, why the hell not.

"Nope, no problem here. Cauldron is just needing to yell a little at someone since he's been all alone for a week," I said with a lazy shrug.

"It's CALDER, fucker!" He bellowed at me, regaining my attention for a brief second.

"That's what I said...Cauldron," I said as I barely concealed a smirk, purposely continuing to call him the wrong name.

He whipped his head around to look at Bishop angrily, his nostrils flaring wildly.

"You better do something with that smart-ass little shit before my guys and I do, Bishop!" He growled, making me pop up an eyebrow, unable to conceal my amusement any longer.

"Are you threatening one of my guards, Havard?" Bishop asked, crossing his arms as he stared at him with a hard stare.

"I don't do threats, Bishop, I make promises and I keep them! So put this guard here on a short leash because my patience is wearing thin!" He shouted angrily before he stomped back to the table with the two guys who had nodded in my direction, sitting down heavily with them. Neither of them had taken their eyes off of our exchange I had noted during Blondie and I's little one-sided chat. That had seemed to be analyzing me the entire time from what I had seen from my peripheral.

Bishop turned to me with a serious look, making me watch him and wait for the little lecture I knew I would be getting.

"Darby, I'm warning you. I have never seen him so pissed in the time he's been here thus far, not even with Enzo. Whatever you did or are doing to piss him off, you should probably stop because it could get you killed," he fretted.

I chuckled at Bishop's worried words, not feeling all that threatened, merely amused at the entirety of it all.

"I haven't done a damn thing to him. I've spoken no more than twelve words to him on the first day which were to tell him to keep quiet, that it didn't matter who he was, and that he didn't need to worry about who I was after he asked me. I only spoke to him after I pulled him away from the other guy, that's it. He's mainly pissed off because I won't say anything to him or even acknowledge him," I said, still chuckling at the absurdity of it all.

I watched Bishop furrow his brows at my words.

"Really? That's it?" He asked, seemingly not believing what I was saying.

I nodded and then chuckled a bit more as a smirk curved its way onto my lips.

"Yeah and, I mean, calling him Cauldron also probably pissed him off too, but oh well. He's a grown man, he'll get over it," I said with a shrug.

"For your sake, you better hope so," Bishop said with a shake of his head.

Interested?

Calder's POV -

As I walked away from that new guard, Derby or Darby or whatever the fuck his name was, I couldn't keep the boiling rage in me from trying to slower simmer up and out of me. The dumb fuck doesn't know who I am or who he's dealing with.

I made it to the table where my two best friends, basically my brothers, were sitting, watching my every move curiously. If only I could think clearly enough to greet them and hear what else is new after being locked up in that damn black box for a week.

"What the fuck was that?" Bo asked in bafflement.

"What the fuck are you talking about?!" I snapped at him angrily as I sat heavily down on the unoccupied third bench at our usual table.

"Woah, man! Calm the fuck down! We were just trying to figure out why you were so damn pissed," Gunnar said, and through his attempt at easing me, I could see his amusement.

Bastard.

"It's that new mother fucking guard!" I all but snarled, jerking my head somewhat in his direction. I didn't even feel like looking at him right now I was so mad.

"What about him? He didn't even say anything to you," Bo said with a raised brow, his bafflement slowly turning to amusement as well.

Bastards, both of them.

"Exactly! I was talking to him and he didn't say anything! And the fucker said my damn name wrong!" I growled, feeling my hands clench into tight fists on the tabletop as I remembered our interaction if it could even be considered that.

Bo and Gunnar looked at each other with smirks on their faces, unable to hide their amusement any longer, only serving to rile me up again.

"What'd he call you?" Gunnar asked eagerly.

"Fucking Cauldron!" I spat out the word.

Then my two supposed best friends, my brothers, busted out laughing like it was the funniest shit that they'd ever heard. I don't think I've ever been as pissed off in my entire life as I was right at this minute.

"That shit's not fucking funny!" I snarled.

"No... because it's fucking hilarious!" Bo howled and hooted out, Gunnar matching him with his own laughter as they went back to their hyena impressions.

Having had enough of their little scene, I angrily banged my fists on the table, making them stop laughing immediately at the loud, echoing sound that resonated around us, causing a few heads to turn momentarily before looking away quickly after I shot them all a menacing glare.

"Alright, damn!" Gunnar huffed in annoyance but otherwise completely calmed. Of course, neither of them was phased by my outburst.

I glared hard at them for a moment more before looking back over my shoulder to see that new fucking guard talking to Bishop. He suddenly laughed at something Bishop said which had his face lighting up slightly, a complete change from his previous bored, stoic face. He looked fucking stunning with his smile, even if I knew it wasn't a full one.

Wait, what the fuck?! Why the hell am I thinking of sissy shit like this, like some fucking lovesick fool?! He's a guy who has a cock, the same as me, not a pussy. I like pussy!

"Calder!" Gunnar and Bo called loudly.

My head quickly snapped back around to see both of them looking at me, perplexed. They both seemed to be studying me, looking for some kind of answer to their silent questions which irked me.

"What?" I grumbled, averting my eyes so I wouldn't have to see their calculating gazes.

"You were just staring at the new guard for like five minutes," Gunnar said, brows furrowed in confusion.

"No, I wasn't!" I denied. There was no way in hell I was staring at him for that long. Hell, I wasn't even staring at him. I was lost in my own thoughts, zoned out, and my face just happened to be pointed in his direction. I wasn't staring at him.

"Um, yeah you were!" Bo said, looking at me like I was mental which resulted in a harsh glare being sent both his and Gunnar's way, but they merely shrugged it off.

"Glampaðu allt sem þú vilt, en við vitum hvað við sáum," Gunnar scoffed at me, a slight smirk just barely pulling up the corners of his mouth.(Glare all you want, but we know what we saw.)

"Fjandinn!" I growled, rising from the table, and moving to storm off.(Fuck off!)

"Where are you going?" Bo asked, making me pause in my departure to turn back around to look at them.

"To my cell," I said flatly, then continued my way up to my cell that was located on the second floor, on the right side yet in the middle of the row of doors that lined the wall.

Upon arriving at my cell, I opened the door and let it slam closed behind me. I walked slowly over to my bed and lay down on it, putting my arms behind my head as I stared up at the ceiling, letting my thoughts swirl around in my mind.

What the fuck is wrong with me? Why would I notice how damn good he looked when he laughed? Why is it him, period, when I've always been interested in hers?

I think I'm finally losing it after having been here for five years out of my thirty-year sentence. I was in for murder, drugs, and a shit load of other charges too. It'd be at least a month if I got into all the shit I've got racked up on my extensive criminal record, so I'll spare all of that. Being here for so long is the only explanation for why I suddenly find another male attractive when I never have before. I've been in here too long without a good pussy to fuck, and a pretty damn useless right hand.

I'm just going to ignore this shit because it's probably only temporary anyway since there haven't been any new guys in here in ages. He's just a new face that I'm not accustomed to yet. Besides, that doesn't matter. I'm still fucking pissed off that he fucking leg swept me, knocking me down to the ground. I don't even know how the fuck he did it since I'm at least twice his size. I'm going to focus on my anger for him taking me down and nothing else...hopefully.

\- ONE MONTH LATER -

It's been a full month since Darby first started working at Terminus. Remember when I said I would do nothing but focus on being pissed at him for taking me down during the riot, and not even bother with any other thoughts?

Yeah, that shit went out the window after the first fucking week. All I can fucking think about is him and it's freaking me the fuck out. If I'm not careful, my dick goes hard from just looking at the little shit. Damn him!

A few weeks ago he broke up a fight between one of my guys and another guy from the dumb-fuck, Enzo's Mafia, and he let out this annoyed growl type of sound as he dragged my guy off of dumb-fuck Enzo's before dragging my guy to his cell for an early lock-up as a punishment. I shit you not, my cock went hard instantly.

I freaked the hell out when it happened, too. I went back to my cell for a lock-up of my own and didn't come out for the rest of the night because I was afraid that if I saw him, my fucked up mind would recall that growl and I'd be fucked all over again with another raging boner.

I don't fucking get it because I'm not gay! I've never even thought of another guy in a sexual way. Hell, just thinking of other guys grosses me the fuck out. But when it comes to Darby, I'm out of my damn mind. I'm not against gays at all, hell, I've got quite a few guys in my Mafia who are gay or bisexual or part of the LGBTQ+ community and have no problem with it. Their sexual preference is none of my business, it's just who they are. But the fact that I'm going hard for a guy is both confusing and alarming to me.

"Okay, what the fuck is going on with you lately?" Gunnar asked as we were sitting at our usual table, playing cards since there is practically nothing to do. We've already been out in the yard earlier in the day and worked out with some of the limited equipment we were given. We couldn't have certain pieces of equipment since they could be used as weapons, but then again, anything could be used as a weapon if you knew how to make it and use it as one.

As I looked up at the clock on the wall that hung over the top of the door, I noted that there was about an hour before the guards' shift changed, meaning the night guards would come in to end the day.

Do you see this shit? Normally I wouldn't give a flying fuck about shift change or what time it was, but now I do because of that sexy little shit!

Oh look, I called him sexy, that's a fucking new one! Wonder what else my damn brain will come up with about him today, nothing will even surprise me anymore since I've apparently lost my sanity.

"What are you talking about? Hit me," I asked, playing dumb as Bo gave me another card. We were playing Blackjack or 21, whatever you know it as, and I'd be damned if I let them know about my current mental state that was in complete disarray as of late. So, feigning innocence was my go-to, not only today but for the vast majority of the past month.

"Don't play stupid. You know what we're talking about. Hit me," Bo said, not buying my lie. Which fucking sucks because I should have known better. They both know me almost as well as I know myself, except for this mysterious new part of me. No one knew or needed to know about it, but I knew I would be spilling it eventually. I was hoping it would be later than sooner.

"No, I don't know. Hold," I said, continuing to try and brush them off as I've been doing much more frequently as of late. It was no wonder why they were both fed up with my obvious bullshit.

"Whatever. I don't know what is going on with you, but ever since Kelby started here, you've been acting weird as fuck. Damn, I busted," Gunnar groaned as he dropped his cards on the table showing 22 as he leaned back in irritation.

"Yeah right. I have n-"

"Cut the shit, Calder! What the hell is going on?!" Bo shouted, catching me by surprise.

I snapped my head around to look at Bo, pissed that he had cut me off when I had been speaking. I was also mildly surprised by his anger directed toward me since he was always such a jokester. Hearing how deadly serious he was showed how fed up with my shit he was, and how screwed I was.

"I told you - both of you - that I'm fucking fine, now lay off!" I shouted as I slammed my cards down and stood up, turning and leaving Gunnar and Bo to stare after me, both extremely confused at how irritated I had become so quickly. Even for me.

There was no way in hell I was voicing my inner turmoil. Why the hell would I want to showcase my sudden change in sexuality or whatever was going on with me? I couldn't explain something to them when I myself didn't know what was going on. Hell, I didn't even want to acknowledge it, but you can see just how well that's gone.

I walked up the stairs that led to the second level where my cell was and just leaned heavily on the railing out in front of my cell. I looked down at the first floor, glaring hard at nothing in particular as I was consumed by my thoughts, as was my new normal since his arrival.

I see and get why they're so confused. I know I've been off and I have been avoiding it, but I can't let them know why, at least, not yet. I need to try and get a handle on things before I share with them my internal struggle. Plus I have no idea how they'll react to my sudden preference change, though I don't know if it could even be considered that.

I looked at the clock seeing that it was time for shift change, then my gaze moved over to the doors that the guards came and left through for shift change. Just like clockwork, in walked Darby with the same stoic and bored look on his face that he wore the vast majority of the time.

I stared at him, watching him closely. I don't know what it was, but there was something different about him today than there was normally. It looked like there was a bit more annoyance and irritation on his face, even though he was trying to keep it concealed with his favorite facial expressions.

The fact that I could read him, and notice such a subtle difference in the way he looked just goes to show that I spend too much time just staring at him. Trying to convince myself not to was like trying to pull teeth from a toothless baby. You just couldn't do it. Like right now, for instance, I was staring hard at him and I couldn't seem to pull my eyes away from him. He captured all of my attention without even trying, and he never even knew it.

Suddenly, he stopped walking midstep to the guard's little private room. He turned around, his eyes instantly moving up and locking on me, making my heart race for multiple reasons.

Fuck! He caught me staring!

A Series of Unfortunate Events

Darby's POV -

Today has been fucking horrendous. I mean, it's just been absolutely awful.

First, the hot water heater in my apartment building is broken so I was forced to take a fucking ice bath so I didn't smell or look like shit. After I took a shower in Antarctica, I went to my kitchen to make myself an omelet but my fucking stove won't turn on, so I had to eat stale ass cereal that I'd had for like a year because I didn't have anything else that didn't require the use of a stove to make. I called maintenance for my apartment building, and after waiting for the fat, lazy bastard to waddle up the stairs to my apartment, he said I'll have to buy a whole new stove and oven since it wasn't covered in my damn rental agreement. That's like three thousand dollars or more!

Oh, did you think that was it? Funny, because it's not.

I was pissed and in a bad mood about my ice bath, and broken stove, so I decided to walk my ass to my couch to watch something on TV to try and calm down, but when I went to turn on the TV it wouldn't turn on. The TV remote control worked since it was lighting up, but did my TV? NO, OF COURSE NOT! So I also need a new fucking TV, too, which is another couple hundred for a decent one! The icing on top of the cake of shit that is my day today? I went to get my uniform for work from out of the dryer, but as I put it on, it felt different. Want to know why? BECAUSE THE MOTHER FUCKER SHRUNK!

I'm so damn over today. I just want to sleep the rest of it away. Too damn bad for me though because I have work and I can't afford to miss any of it, especially now that I have to buy a shit ton of new things for me to be able to function.

Walking into the unit, I tried to hide my annoyance from not only the day but from the fact that my pants were squeezing the fuck out of my ass, my dick, and my damn balls too. By the end of my shift, I know I'm going to have lost feelings in all three. As it was, the pants were digging into my ass, and with each step, the front tightened so much that I worried I'd blow the crotch out of them, and give everyone a fucking peep show.

As I moved in further, nearing the guard's room, I could feel someone staring at me causing me to pause, turn around slightly, and look up. I was quick to spot the culprit. Calder. He was leaning against the railing, staring directly at me without blinking. For a second it looked like a flash of panic was on his face, but then he turned and walked off, leaving me left looking at where he last stood. Seeing him 'panic' was probably my imagination since he was a ways away from me, so I didn't think anything of it.

I turned back around and continued to head to the guards' office, thinking about Calder and how his staring was becoming a regular occurrence. It's not the first time I've noticed him staring at me, but I normally don't look back at him when he does, yet today I did. His staring was annoying as all hell, and it kind of made me uncomfortable with how often he did it.

I scanned my identification badge and opened the door, walking into the office where the day shift officers were getting their stuff together and talking amongst themselves. I couldn't help but overhear a couple of nearby officers since they weren't exactly quiet in their conversation.

"Hey, have you noticed how weird Havard's been acting over the last month?" One of the day or morning shift guards, Guard Tennison - a large mocha-colored man with dark eyes and a buzzcut, deep brown hair who was in his late fifties - asked another guard from his shift.

"Yeah, I have. He doesn't do shit anymore. He used to always pick fights over dumb shit and just be an overall asshole, but now he just kind of keeps to himself. It's weird as hell," Guard Milner - a man who was also the same skin tone and age as Guard Tennison - replied.

"I know. I wonder if another riot will break out?" Guard Tennison grumbled with a touch of hope in his voice, grabbing the last of his things from his locker and turning. That's how fucked up Terminus and its occupants, as well as staff, are. Hoping to experience a fight? That's fucked up. But honestly, I was a little bit too, because at times it got boring as hell.

"Who knows? Might make shit interesting around here again. Now it's just boring as fuck," Guard Milner said, doing the same and also sounding hopeful. See, I definitely belong here.

Upon turning around and noticing me standing at my own locker, they nodded which I reciprocated as I put my stuff in my locker, watching as they left from my peripheral.

All any of the guards have been talking about lately is Calder and how, basically, well-behaved he is. Apparently, he used to be in and out of isolation multiple times a month for fighting the other inmates and, on occasion, the guards too. I don't think they should be complaining, because maybe he finally learned his lesson or something and is resigned to his fate of being stuck here for the duration of his sentence.

I was pulled from my thoughts by the sound of catcalls and wolf whistles.

"Damn, who's the one with the ass?" Patrick called with an obvious grin in his voice I could easily detect from his tone alone.

"We finally get a girl in here with us?" Ryan asked excitedly.

I had my head behind my locker door, obscuring my face as placed my stuff in my locker, checking my phone for any messages, though at their words I was quick to put it down. If there's a female guard in here with an ass like they're describing, I sure as shit want to see it for myself. I pulled my head back around the corner of my opened locker door to see both Patrick and Ryan looking at me, completely appalled as they looked at me, while Bishop laughed loudly from where he was standing near the computer monitors.

"Oh, that shit was priceless! You guys were eyeing up Darby's ass!" Bishop hooted in amusement, letting out a belly laugh.

I couldn't help but roll my eyes and snort. That was not what I was expecting, but I should have known because of how tight these damn pants are on me.

"Did you two enjoy the show?" I joked, shutting my locker door as I smirked at them, unable to hold back my own amusement despite my earlier sour mood.

"In our defense, those pants are tight as hell and we couldn't see that it was you!" Ryan attempted to defend himself and Patrick, both of their cheeks dusted in a faint pink.

"Is no one going to acknowledge the fact that, guy or not, he's got a great ass? Just saying," Patrick asked once his cheeks lessened in color, raising his hands in the air as a form of defense against what he had said.

"Thanks, I guess, Patrick," I chuckled with a shake of my head. I didn't really know what to say in response to that, but I guess it was a compliment.

"What happened to your pants in the first place? Because I know they weren't that tight before. They're too damn noticeable to miss seeing... that," Bishop asked once his chuckles had subsided.

"My entire uniform shrunk in the damn dryer today and I have no idea how. I just hope that's not about to quit on me too," I said as I thought that maybe my washing machine, dryer, or both, could be about to quit working, too, adding yet another high cost for me to worry about. I groaned at the thought, rubbing my face in frustration at the reminder of my shitty day.

"Hey, you okay Darby? You seem kind of stressed," Ryan noted.

"Probably because I am," I snorted humorlessly.

"Why, what's going on?" Patrick asked in sudden concern, both Bishop and Ryan's faces contorting to match his, concerned looks being thrown at me from them now too.

"Today is just one of those days from hell where everything that could go wrong has," I explained, leaning back against the locker next to mine, tilting my head back to rest against it as I closed my eyes.

"That bad, huh?" Bishop questioned, already sounding sympathetic despite not knowing what I had experienced today.

"Yeah. The hot water heater in my building is broken so I had to take a fucking arctic shower before coming here, then my stove and oven decided that they don't want to work anymore so I need to buy a new one of those, next my TV said it wanted to add to my ever-growing list of things that want to drive me insane since it also stopped working today, and then, as has already been noted, my uniform shrunk in the dryer," I elaborated on my lovely day, still keeping my eyes closed to stave off the oncoming headache.

"Fuck, that really does sound awful," Ryan whistled lowly.

"Are you gonna be okay?" Patrick asked me, but I just shrugged as I lifted my head off of the locker while meeting their eyes.

"I'll survive."

"Why not ask your parents for help or ask to stay with them?" Bishop asked, making me tense at the mere mention of my parents. Thankfully, no one seemed to notice, or if they did, they didn't say anything about it which made me grateful for that.

"They don't live in Nevada. I'm originally from Denver, Colorado so that's where they are," I said, not providing any more information aside from that.

"Okay, well, if you ever need anything, don't hesitate to ask us, okay? We're here for you," Bishop said, sending me a smile that I returned with a small one of my own as I nodded at them.

"Okay. And thanks, guys. I appreciate it, I really do," I said as I stood up straight against the lockers, closing my own locker door.

"Alright, enough of this sappy shit, let's get to work!" Ryan announced with a wide grin, ever the one to break an emotion-heavy atmosphere, for which I was grateful.

We all nodded, Patrick and Ryan, moving to go sit in the two chairs to watch the cameras while Bishop and I walked to the door to head out to the main area to patrol. He opened the door and walked out with me following behind him, pulling the door closed behind me.

Bishop stayed on the left side of the unit while I went off to the right side, walking slowly as I watched the inmates, checking to see if they were up to no good, on the verge of fighting, or just talking of doing anything of that sort. You know, my classic duties as a Penitentiary guard.

I made it about halfway around on my side, and so far nothing was out of the ordinary that I'd seen or heard. I got closer to Calder's normal table where he usually sat with the same two guys, but only the two guys were there, so Calder was probably still up in his cell as he usually was.

A hard smack cracked semi-painfully against the center of my ass which was followed by someone grabbing a handful of my ass, squeezing it immediately after the slap.

Great, today just keeps getting BETTER!

Protection With A Price

A hard smack cracked semi-painfully against the center of my ass which was followed by someone grabbing a handful of my ass, squeezing it immediately after the slap.

I quickly spun around, about to take the now laughing inmate down for his little stunt, when out of nowhere, Calder appeared in what could only be described as a blind rage. He snapped the guy up by the neck, hand tightly wrapped around his throat as he lifted him clean off of his feet. Then he suddenly slammed him down on the ground, back of the head first, in the span of a second, maybe even less. It happened so fucking fast that my eyes barely caught the movement. The sound of the guy's head connecting with the concrete ground of the unit echoed disturbingly loudly throughout the main area, quickly followed by his scream of agony that left the entire unit, which was previously abuzz with noise from the voices of the inmates, dead silent.

I snapped out of my shock upon having realized that it was my job to keep inmates from killing one another instead of watching it happen before my eyes, no matter how traumatic the sight was. I surged forward, grabbing both of Calder's forearms, jerking him off and away from the wailing guy as I called out for backup. You would think that after the silence that echoed throughout the normally noisy unit, or the haunting cry that was easily audible, guards would be rushing over on their own.

Apparently not.

"Bishop! I need medical assistance immediately!" I shouted as I continued to drag Calder's large, muscled body back from the guy whilst he struggled against my hold, attempting to go back after the heavily bleeding inmate. His wails had quickly quieted a few seconds after the initial impact as he was losing consciousness almost as quickly as he was losing blood which was pouring out from the back of his head as if someone had turned on a bathtub's faucet.

Bishop finally ran over, looking at the inmate on the ground - he was now loosely holding his head as blood poured down the back of it and pooling underneath him, the color of his skin quickly paling - in shock.

"Kelby, what the fuck happened?!" Bishop asked in confusion, sounding horrified as well as he was unable to remove his eyes from the scene before us.

I went to respond to his question when Calder began to shout and snarl angrily, jerking roughly at the firm hold I had on him. He was surely going to have bruises from my fingers from how hard I was holding and squeezing his large forearms.

"The fucker got handsy with him so I taught him a fucking lesson! Touch him again bitch, and I'll rip out your fucking throat and shove it up your ass!" He was screaming so loudly and was so enraged that his normally pale, almost cream-colored skin was now a bright red.

Calder continued to struggle in my hold, somehow managing to free one arm from my bruising grip which resulted in me quickly giving him a repeat of just over a month ago as I brought him to his knees. I knocked his feet out from under him, locked his arms tightly behind his back, and then quickly moved to grab my handcuffs that I kept on one of my belt loops, locking them around both of his wrists to further secure him.

"Kelby, get him up to his cell and lock him in!" Bishop ordered.

"Got it, Bishop," I said with a curt nod of understanding.

"Why am I getting in trouble for helping a guard?! The fucker sexually assaulted him and I protected him!" Calder hollered.

"Let's go, up!" I shouted at him to get him to hear me over his own shouts. I pulled him to his feet and began to drag him off toward his cell when his two friends jumped in front of me. I growled lowly as I glared at them, my irritation levels steadily rising. "Unless you two want to go to your cells early tonight, I suggest you both fucking move."

"Let him fucking go you son of a b-" His dark chocolate-haired, indigo blue-eyed friend who had two full-sleeve tattoos of some kind of almost tribal designs, Gunnar, began but was soon cut off by Calder who spoke in an unfamiliar, foreign language.

"Ljúktu við setninguna, Gunnar, og ég slá tennurnar niður í hálsinn á þér," even with him speaking in another language, I could hear the threat in his words.(Finish that sentence, Gunnar, and I knock your teeth down your fucking throat.)

"Af hverju fjandinn ekki?! Þú varst að hjálpa honum!" His other friend, Bo, whose hair was a lighter brown with blue-green eyes, cried out angrily.(Why the fuck not?! You were helping him!)

"Það verður í lagi með mig. Ég skal útskýra í annað skiptið, en farðu bara af stað og láttu hann fara með mig í klefa minn," Calder said with a stern edge to the odd-sounding words that seemed to flow from his mouth with ease.(I'll be fine. I'll explain some other time, but just back off and let him take me to my cell.)

"Svo þú ert loksins að fara að segja okkur?" Gunnar asked, quirking a brow at Calder in what looked like mild exasperation.(So you're finally going to tell us?)

I don't know what the fuck they're saying but I'm done playing games. I felt like I was caught in the middle of some kind of foreign pinball game between the three of them as they went back and forth with each other, leaving me lost and annoyed.

"Okay, that's it! Let's go, all three of you to your cells!" I shouted, tugging Calder while making a motion to the other two to get a move on to their cells that were also upstairs and near his.

"Já! Færðu þig núna!" Calder snapped at them, whatever small bit of patience he had with them snapping.(Yes! Now move!)

Whatever Calder had said to them had them throwing their hands up in surrender as they slowly backed away, but they still didn't seem too happy to be doing so. Like I gave a fuck about how they felt about it, it's my damn job!

"Okay, fine! You win, we're backing off!" Bo spoke first, a slight glare easily detected in his eyes.

"Yeah, we don't want any problems!" Gunnar finished, waving his hands at me in an attempt to placate me.

I glared at them as I pushed Calder forward. As we walked past them, heading up the stairs to his cell, I made sure to keep on high guard to see if the two of them decided to pull some kind of stunt in an effort to free Calder that could result in me getting attacked. Thankfully, they stayed where they were, and I had no trouble hauling him up the stairs to the second floor.

When we got to his cell, I moved around him, opening up his cell door, only for his foot to quickly shoot up. He kicked the door closed before spinning me around and pinning me to his cell door, getting right up in my face with his hands placed on either side of my head. The fucker had boxed me in, giving me no place to go.

Wait, his hands?! But the handcuffs were on him!

"You didn't honestly think I didn't know how to get out of a little pair of handcuffs, did you? I'm a Mafia boss for fucks sake! I can get out of anything, anywhere, at any time I want to!" Calder smirked with a dark chuckle.

My heart pounded roughly against my ribs at the fact that he not only had me pinned to the door but he was pressing up against me too. The close proximity between us was making my body go a little haywire. I think there's something wrong with me because I should probably be scared or at least worried, but I'm not.

"If that's true, then what are you still doing in here? Because from what I've heard, you've been here for five years now and this place isn't exactly a five-star hotel," I spat back at him, deciding to press his buttons even more since he can apparently 'get out whenever he wants to'. If that was the case, why would he stay in here for as long as he had?

"This is a break from my regular work schedule. Besides, I was going to bust out soon, but I've decided to stick around a bit more," he said with the smirk still smeared across his lips.

"So a vacation? Not something someone who's in jail would normally say, but whatever. That's your choice. What's keeping you from leaving?" I asked, wanting to keep him talking so I could try and think of a way to get myself out of this mess and catch him while he was off guard like I had done twice before.

He leaned in closer to me, getting so close that his nose brushed against mine, making my eyes widen in shock at our close proximity. A flicker of something passed through his eyes that had a shiver running down my spine. But just as every other time, it moved so quickly that it was gone before I had the chance to try and pinpoint what it meant.

"A certain new guard has my attention, and I've decided I want to stick around. Find out more about him," he breathed out against my lips.

Holy fuck, is he flirting with me?! Why am I letting him?! And why am I fucking enjoying it?!

This is wrong. I don't like guys, I like girls and only girls. Sure my last fuck was shit but not every fuck will be mind blow-

My thoughts immediately evaporated into thin air when he surged forward, smashing his lips against mine, and sucking my bottom lip into his mouth, the feeling was nothing short of amazing. A moan slipped between my lips, earning me a groan from between his. Another shot of something ran down my spine, going down to my toes.

Fuck, what the hell am I doing right now?! It's a HE kissing me, not a SHE!

As I realized what exactly was happening, I pushed the feeling aside as I shoved him off of me, quickly spinning around and successfully pulling myself away from him. In an instant, I was opening his cell door and driving him inside, taking my cuffs from his hand all in one fluid motion. I slammed the door shut, quickly inserting my key into the lock and twisting it so it was locked, preventing him from exiting for the rest of the night.

"You can't tell me you didn't enjoy that!" He called through the door to me. When I made the mistake of looking up at him, I saw a wide smirk on his lips that was shining with saliva that I hoped belonged to himself.

"Shut the fuck up! That didn't happen and it shouldn't have happened! Enjoy your early night in, CAULDRON!" I snapped in hopes of pissing him off, but instead, he laughed at me. A full, head-tossed back deep, rumbling laugh.

"After that kiss, I definitely will! I can't wait until tomorrow!" He called back, shooting me a seductive wink.

I hurried off in a panic, hearing his loud laughter following me down the hall. Before I reached the stairs, I looked below my belt, gawking as I saw the major boner I was sporting.

"Mother fucker! Now is not the time for this!" I muttered quietly, stress seeping from my words like water from a wrung-out sponge. I was struggling to find things to think of that would make me go soft because I couldn't stop thinking about Calder and that damn kiss! "Fuck, I need to go to a club with Grant on one of my days off for some good pussy."

I fucking kid you not, the moment that I muttered 'pussy' my cock went soft as if it had never been hard in the first place.

WHAT THE FUCK?!

I hurried down the stairs, pissed off to the highest degree, as I headed straight to the guard's office. I quickly scanned my badge, pulling the door open just enough for me to slip through before pulling it closed behind me and bolting inside.

"What's got you running, Darby?" Patrick chuckled as I hurried past him and Ryan who was also chuckling at my rapid pace.

"I have to take a piss real bad," I lied as I ran straight into the bathroom while doing my best to conceal anything that could potentially give them a hint to what had just transpired. Instead, I only heard their chuckles get louder as they genuinely believed I needed a piss. Good.

I locked the single stall door, barely able to even think straight as I quickly unbuckled, unbuttoned, and unzipped my pants, pulling them and my boxers down to my knees as I looked down at my soft cock with a hard stare.

"Pussy! I like a nice, wet, tight, pussy!" I hissed down at my cock as quietly as possible so no one would hear my odd little chant, but nothing happened. Not even a twitch.

Another thought popped into my head and figured I might as well try it even if I don't like the outcome because I needed to know. I closed my eyes, inhaling a long breath before looking back down at my cock, letting out a shaky breath as my nerves spiked. I hissed down at my cock again, continuing to do so as quietly as possible.

"Calder. Calder kissing me."

Sure enough, the fucker went hard. Hard. As. Damn. Steel.

I lightly banged my forehead on the wall, closing my eyes and letting out a low groan that quickly morphed into an even lower growl as I came to a sudden, infuriating realization.

"That mother fucker broke my dick!"

Distracted

Last night - well, early this morning is more like it - I got home and again tried to test out my cock. In an effort to get hard, I even tried watching the porn I've always watched which had always gotten me hard as fuck, but it didn't work. But guess what did?

Just saying HIS name made me go hard. Even thinking about him right now was making me go hard which was not a good thing since I was parking in the lot in front of the Penitentiary for yet another shift with the bastard himself.

I groaned and beat my head on my steering wheel a few times in sheer frustration.

"You. Stupid. Fucking. Criminal. Why? Why?! WHY?!" I groaned.

I thought of pussy which immediately made me soft which I hated. Not so much ridding myself of the boner I had before going to work since that was a good thing. I didn't need any more attention from psychopathic criminals. No, I hated that the thought of girls and pussy now turned me off instead of turning me on like it always had before.

After taking a few calming breaths, I checked the time and saw that I needed to get out of my car to head inside right now or I would risk being late. So, I got out of the car and went inside, taking my sweet time to get back to the unit, regardless of my near tardiness since I was on my way to my normal post. When I did get to my section and entered the building, I hurried to the guard's office, keeping my eyes locked on the office door, watching for the green light that signaled it had unlocked as I swiped my badge. When the light flashed, I opened the door and walked in, pulling it closed behind me.

"What's up, Darby, how was your day today? Any better than yesterday?" Patrick asked, shooting me a grin, always the first to greet me.

"Hmm? Oh, yeah, I had a better day," I hummed, my mind elsewhere. Obviously.

"You good?" Ryan asked me, easily noting my wandering thoughts as he watched me closely.

"Yeah, I'm fine why?" I said, attempting to play it all off. I did not need him to see something. I didn't want to be questioned by anyone, not with how close I felt to biting someone's head off.

"You just seem a little distracted today. You were a little distracted yesterday, too, after you came out of the bathroom," Ryan elaborated on his observation of me.

Well, yeah, because one of the fucking inmates kissed me and basically admitted to having feelings for me. But I can't tell anyone that, otherwise, I'll lose my job. I actually liked working here, and I was starting to like the guys I worked with, too, surprisingly enough. There was no way I was going to let Calder and his little games ruin this job for me. Not a chance in hell.

"Yeah, just worried about buying a new oven and TV for my apartment," I said, which wasn't a total lie, but it was not at the forefront of my mind and hadn't been since before yesterday's shift.

"Well, I'll keep an eye out for a cheap TV and oven for you," Patrick said, sending me a smile.

"Thanks, I appreciate it," I thanked him with a slight smile and a nod back.

Just then, Bishop walked in, looking around until his eyes landed on me, looking a little relieved oddly enough.

"Alright, good you're here. Come on, it's time to start our watch in the main area," Bishop said, nodding his head back behind him, signaling me to hurry it up and follow him for the normal evening patrol.

"Yeah, okay, I'm coming," I said, trying to sound as nonchalant as I possibly could.

Fuck! I don't want to go out there! What if I look at him and I go hard?! How the fuck am I supposed to explain that?!

Regardless, I didn't have time to think about it too much or a choice in staying in the office because I was already walking out behind Bishop, keeping my facial expression the same as it always was: stoic. Not a single emotion aside from boredom on my face, even though I'm not really bored. More like I'm nervous as all hell. And still a little pissed about yesterday and the balls that bastard had to pull that little stunt.

The annoying yet rational part of my brain was yelling at me that it was because of a certain inmate that I was becoming more and more interested in the Penitentiary and the job which was the reason why the boredom on my face was now a mask. Now I was just nervous, yet I fought to ignore it as I walked alongside Bishop, deciding to make conversation with him instead of waiting for him to start up a conversation with me.

"So how is the inmate whose head was busted open by Calder yesterday?" I asked, finding difficulty in both saying his name and keeping myself soft.

"He's got a concussion and a few staples in his head to keep it together. He's also got a small fracture in his skull," Bishop said making me wince at his condition.

"Damn, he really did a number on him," I muttered out, more to myself, but loud enough for Bishop to have heard.

"Yeah, he sure did," he agreed, going silent for a moment before speaking once more. "Hey, I checked the security footage from yesterday."

Fuck, here it goes! He saw Calder kissing me on the security footage and now I'm getting fired! Fuck you, you blonde asshole! You just cost me my job and you are for sure going to get your balls shoved back up inside you for it!

Even though I was freaking the fuck out on the inside right now, I didn't let it show on the outside. I remained calm, cool, and collected, despite my constant internal panic that was gradually rising by the millisecond. Maybe if I acted as if nothing had happened, he'll think he was seeing things.

Fat chance of that happening.

"Oh, yeah?" I said casually.

"Yeah. I wanted to know what led up to the incident so I could file the report. I have to say, even on the footage, I don't know where the fuck he came from, but he was pissed the fuck off," Bishop said, sounding mystified and awed.

Oh, thank fuck. That's all it was about, now I can relax a little.

"Yeah, me neither. Is he in isolation now because of what he did yesterday?" I asked, silently hoping and praying that Bishop would say yes, just so I wouldn't have to see him today or maybe even for a few days if luck was on my side.

"No. Because of the fact that he came and was helping you, a guard, he got let off with a warning," Bishop said, making my heart sink.

Mother fucker! Why couldn't the big guy in the sky just help me out this once? I don't ask for much from Him!

As I was panicking in my head, I felt a set of eyes on me, practically burning a hole into the side of my head. I already knew whose they were without looking, and yet, my dumbass still turned my head and looked right dead at him. Sure enough, he was staring right dead at me. His lips, which had been in a straight line when I first looked at him, were now slightly curled up as he smirked at me before sending me another wink like the one from yesterday, making me look away quickly.

But the damage was already done because I had noticed the two guys that were sitting with him look between the both of us in shock right before I had fully turned away. I could feel my pants getting even fucking tighter than the damn things already were from being shrunk as a sudden unwanted situation began to arise in my pants. I quickly thought of the one thing that now seemed to always make me go soft.

Pussy. Pussy. Pussy.

And there went my hard-on as it worked like a charm. Thank the heavens!

Wait, no not like-

"You good, Darby?" Bishop questioned, quickly snapping my eyes up to look at him from where they had drifted to glare holes into a nearby wall.

"Yeah, why?" I asked, speaking quickly to try and get the attention off of me.

"You seem like something's on your mind," Bishop commented with a shrug, practically repeating what Ryan and Patrick had already said.

Fuck, multiple people were noticing that I was off. Despite it being obvious, I was hoping they'd all be oblivious to it or at least ignore it, but apparently not. Think dumbass, think! What should I say?

"Sorry, it's just these fucking pants are tight as shit!" Again, it's not a total lie but it's not exactly the truth, either. Plus, they were almost even tighter a few minutes ago.

"You know, you can just buy another pair or two up in the office, right?" Bishop asked with a chuckle, making my eyes snap over to meet his.

"Please tell me you're not just screwing with me," I begged him with wide, hopeful eyes. He laughed a bit more with a shake of his head.

"No, I'm not. You can buy them in the front office," he said, and quite frankly that's the best news I've heard all day.

"Why didn't you tell me that yesterday?!" I nearly shouted at him, realizing that one of my problems could have already been fixed.

"Because we had to deal with Calder and the other inmate whose skull he busted open," Bishop said, lifting a brow at me like I was an idiot which to be fair I was.

"Oh yeah. Yeah, that's right," I said, and we both chuckled.

Fuck yes! Something's finally going right! I won't have to keep wearing these tight-ass pants anymore! By this time tomorrow, I will finally have back a pair of comfortable pants! Nothing could take this win from me.

"Good evening Darby. Evening Bishop," a familiar, and unwanted deep voice spoke up from what sounded like a few short feet in front of me.

Aw fuck! Now I've gone and jinxed myself! Great! Just fucking great!

Telling Friends

Calder's POV -

Damn, I can't get that kiss from last night out of my head or the fact that he is strong as fuck despite him being a lot smaller than I am. I never would have thought he would have been able to move me like that, or so fast. It was damn hot, though.

I'm just hoping I can get another kiss from him again tonight because after he left me in my cell last night, I had to jerk myself off. It was the biggest load I've ever let out, even after dreaming and imagining him. Now, I had a real taste of him, and it felt fucking amazing. Afterward, I slept like a fucking baby. It was the greatest sleep I've ever gotten in my life, even before I got locked up. Just envisioning him in my mind was like the sweetest dream, and soothed me all through the night.

When I woke up this morning my mood dimmed slightly as I remembered that I had promised to tell Bo and Gunnar what was going on with me lately back when I was getting dragged up to my cell by Darby last night. I wish I could take my promise back, just to buy myself another day or two, but I know that stalling any further would be impossible. Especially since I had already promised them, they weren't going to let me. They were nearly as stubborn as me at times, probably as a result of the three of us having grown up together.

I'm shit you not when I say that from the moment I walked out of my cell this morning, they were both wanting to know what was going on. Thankfully, I was able to stall a bit longer when I told them that I'd tell them later, which I will, but not just yet. Some kind of small break is better than none at all.

However, right now it was the time I had been anticipating since the night before: it was time for the shift change. I'm sitting at my usual table with Bo and Gunnar, staring daggers at the door, watching and waiting for him to walk through them. All of the other guards had gotten here already, but not him. He was always one of the first, if not the first to get here. I was getting worried that he may not show, and just the thought had my chest aching. I needed him to be here or else I would lose my mind.

And then the door opened, allowing the ache in my chest to ease the moment I saw him. He came walking in, hurrying over to the guards' office. It was the same as he had done the day before but his steps were a little more rushed today as he quickly opened the door and entered inside, not even looking around as he normally would.

I continued to stare at the guard's door, watching as Bishop went into the office after glancing in my direction briefly. Moments later he was coming back out with Darby who was talking to him about something.

I couldn't help but notice the fact that his pants were hugging his ass, legs, and cock tightly. It was no wonder that bastard had made a move on him yesterday, but it didn't mean he needed to. He should have kept his fucking hands to himself. It's not my fault that he was a dumb fuck who needed to be taught a lesson. But God, his ass was better than any girl I've ever been with or known. I honestly don't even give a fuck anymore that he's a guy. I just want him more than anything or anyone else in the world. And I planned on having him, one way or another. He will be mine.

His head turned and his eyes locked on mine, having caught me staring at him again, not that it was hard to do since anymore my eyes rarely left him. There was no use in even trying to play it off either so I continued to stare at him with a smirk, shooting him the same sultry wink as yesterday as I bit the inside of my lip as I let my eyes trail his body. Instead of rushing off as he had recently taken to doing, he instead quickly turned back around to face Bishop.

"What the fuck was that?!" Gunnar hissed lowly at me, instead of shouting like Bo would have done.

I pulled my eyes away from what was mine and looked over to Bo and Gunnar who were both looking at me in complete and utter disbelief. It was quite amusing to see those deranged looks on their faces.

"What was what?" I asked sarcastically, a slight smirk still on my lips as I continued to eye Darby from the corner of my eye. Fuck, even from my peripheral I could see how good he looked. His ass was fucking massive and all I could think of doing was burying myself between his cheeks. Face, fingers, cock, all three, it didn't matter at this point.

"Don't play stupid, Calder! We saw you staring at Kelby, which you've been doing a lot of, but then you winked at him?!" Bo said, his voice surprisingly at a normal level. To be honest, I didn't know that he had a normal level when speaking after hearing his loud voice over the last I don't even know how many years. It was weird, making me prefer his normal ear-bleeding tone.

"Yeah, and?" I said. I wasn't going to deny it any longer. Honestly, this would probably be the best and easiest way for me to tell them since they saw just our little interaction if it could even be called such. If I had my way, I'd have pinned against this table, my tongue making itself at home in his mouth to show everyone who he belonged to. But that wasn't exactly acceptable and would probably piss him off, though I can't say the idea of either option doesn't entice me.

"Og hvað? Ertu eins og að hella honum núna eða eitthvað?" Gunnar asked, switching over to speaking Icelandic since there were very few who understood it in the Penitentiary with us if anyone. The three of us were born and raised in Norway where we were taught to speak Icelandic and Norwegian since we frequently visited Iceland for business and pleasure. We knew both but mainly spoke to each other in Icelandic when we didn't want to be overheard since most of our Mafia members were better at Norwegian than Icelandic. We also spoke quickly so that it was purposely more difficult for us to be understood by any potential eavesdroppers.(So, what? Are you like fucking him now or something?)

"Ekki núna, en ég vona að það verði fljótlega," I said casually, smirking as their eyes went as wide as saucers. But they wore no negative reaction, Bo's next question further proving that.(Not now, but I hope to be soon.)

"Og hvað? Ertu kátur núna?" Bo asked, not seeming upset, just incredibly curious. Probably too curious, knowing him.(So, what? Are you gay now?)

"Nei, af því að hann er eini strákurinn sem ég laðast að eða kyssti af því tilefni," I said, licking my lips as I remembered his delectable taste. I didn't know how to describe it except maybe as Heaven.(No, because he's the only guy I'm attracted to or kissed for that matter.)

"Þú hvað?!" Gunnar and Bo cried out, their voices raising but not enough to attract any attention. Thankfully.(You what?!)

"Ég kyssti hann og skammast mín ekki fyrir að segja að þetta hafi verið frábært," I admitted, shrugging off their shock, having expected it. It was understandable seeing as I had never expressed any previous interest in the same gender of myself. Not until my little guard.(I kissed him, and I'm not ashamed to say it was great.)

"Þegar fjandinn gerðist það?!" Gunnar asked, looking more and more floored by my words.(When the fuck did that happen?!)

"Í gær þegar hann reyndi að koma mér aftur í klefa minn," I said as I bit my bottom lip, a silly grin on my face at how soft his lips were and how good it felt to have his body pinned under mine. Again, it was fucking Heaven.(Yesterday when he tried to put me in my cell.)

"Þú veist að hann gæti misst vinnuna og hvað það sem þú tveir er að gerast verður gert, ekki satt?" Bo said, brow cocked up in mild disapproval.(You know that he could lose his job and whatever shit you two have going on will be done, right?)

"Já, en það mun ekki gerast af því að við lendum ekki í því," I said without a shred of doubt.(Yeah, but that's not going to happen because we won't get caught.)

"Hvað gerir þig svona viss um það?" Gunnar asked, not seeming as certain as I was.(What makes you so sure of that?)

I grinned widely as I wrapped my arms around each of their shoulders and pulled them into my sides, slapping their backs heartily as I looked happily between the two of them.

"Vegna þess að tveir bræður minir ætla að hjálpa mér."(Because my two brothers are going to help me.)

"Af hverju erum við dregin inní þitt undarlega kynlifssamband sem þú vilt eiga við vörðuna?!" Bo whined at me like the child he is. It was hilarious to me that he thought that either he or Gunnar even had a choice in the matter.(Why are we getting dragged into the weird sex relationship you want to have with the guard?!)

"Það vill ekki til. Það mun gerast," I said with one hundred percent certainty.(There's no want to it. It's going to happen.)

"Og veistu hvernig?" Gunnar asked, still not convinced. Him and his damn need to try and get us all to be responsible adults. I don't even know why he tries anymore knowing none of it will work. We're all too damn stubborn and stuck in our ways.(And you know this how?)

"Vegna þess að hann vill hafa mig jafn slæmt og ég vil hafa hann, sama hversu hart hann reynir að neita því, þá getur hann það ekki. Svo, þið tvö að hjálpa mér?" I said, looking between the two of them, unable to fully mask my hope that they would give in to me. If they didn't, I would find some other way because of just how determined I was to have him but with their help, it would make things significantly easier. Plus, I just wanted them to be there by my side like they always are. They're my brothers.(Because he wants me just as bad as I want him, no matter how hard he tries to deny it, he can't. So, will you two help me?)

They looked at each other, having a silent conversation with one another before sighing and looking back at me, nodding their heads in sync.

"Fínt," Bo conceded with a grumble.(Fine.)

"Já! Takk-" I began, only to be cut off.(Yes! Thanks-)

"En við eitt skilyrði," Gunnar cut in, holding his hand up to get me to be quiet. Though the motion irritated me, I let it go because they had agreed to help me.(But on one condition.)

"Hvað? Nefndu það," I said as I sat back, looking at them both to see who would speak next.(What? Name it.)

"Þú segir okkur að þetta sé bara skemmtilegt og ekkert alvarlegt," Bo said making me let out a light huff of disbelief.(You tell us that this is just fun and nothing serious.)

That's easy because that's all it was. Once I got my fill of him and had him out of my system, I would be fine and forget all about him. Though I wanted to know why they wanted me to assure them that it would be.

"Já það er. En af hverju samt? Myndirðu ekki taka við mér efég væri hommi?" I asked, a brow raising, though I already knew that they would be accepting of me. Hell, they already have been, thus far. Gay or not, I wanted to fuck a guy and they weren't overly concerned or disgusted by it.(Yeah, it is. But why, though? Would you not accept me if I was gay?)

"Komdu nú. Þú veist að við myndum gera það," Gunnar scoffed, shaking his head with an exasperated look on his face.(Come on, now. You know we would.)

"Við viljum bara ekki að þú lendir of djúpt og verðir þá hræddur um að einn ykkar vilji meira en bara leyndarmál ríða félaga," Bo explained with a shrug of his own.(We just don't want you getting in too deep and then freaking out if one of you wants more than just secret fuck buddies.)

Now it was my turn to scoff at them.

"Þú þarft ekki að þurfa að hafa áhyggjur af því, þvi það er ekki að gerast," I said with a shake of my head at the ridiculous idea of theirs.(You don't need to worry about that, because that's not happening.)

I heard a deep, yet still at the same time soft, laugh and my head snapped up to see both Bishop and Darby walking this way, chuckling amongst themselves causing a wide grin to cover my lips.

"Ef þið munið afsaka mig. Það er viss vörður sem ég þarf að tala við ... einslega," I smirked as I stood up quickly from the table, pulling my lower lip up between my teeth as I did so.(Now, if you guys will excuse me. There's a certain guard I need to speak to...privately.)

"Góði Guð. Vertu allavega ekki of augljós," Gunnar chuckled, shaking his head in amusement.(Good, God. At least don't be too obvious.)

"Eða hátt!" Bo added in teasingly.(Or loud!)

I rolled my eyes at the two of them, hearing them laugh at each other's little comments as I walked up to Bishop and Darby.

"Good evening Darby. Evening Bishop."

Trapped

Darby's POV -

Stupid fucker! He already broke my damn dick, why can't he just fuck off?!

"Evening Calder. Anything I can help you with?" Bishop asked him while I watched as he looked at me, a slight smirk on his lips.

Nope. Fuck no. I'm leaving before anything happens, I thought to myself as I turned to walk off.

"Actually, I need Officer Kelby's help," Calder called out for me, halting me in my tracks despite my wanting to rush off as inconspicuously as possible.

"Sorry, Havard but whatever it is, I'm sure Bishop can help you with it," I said as I looked at him from over my shoulder while slowly beginning to walk backward once more. There was no way in hell I would willingly go anywhere alone with him. Not after the last time. I would not be making the same mistake twice.

"Yeah, but it's about last night. You dropped your handcuff keys in my cell when you went to leave. I tried to get you to come back for them, but you wouldn't so I held onto them for you. They're up in my cell right now. If you'll come upstairs with me you can get them from where I stored them for safekeeping so no one else knew I had them," Calder said innocently, but the smirk he wore promised he was anything but that. Yet his words had me coming to an immediate stop as I quickly checked the pocket I always kept my handcuff keys. Sure enough, they were gone.

Fuck! Now I'm going to have to go up to his cell with him again! And we'll be alone since everyone is downstairs! Who the fuck knows what stunt he's going to pull on me this time around?! He planned this shit, I know he did!

"Yeah, I'd go get those and quick, Darby. While you're up there, I want you to do a search of his cell to make sure he doesn't have anything else that he shouldn't, like contraband of any kind," Bishop said.

The more Bishop spoke, the broader Calder's smirk got while my heart raced faster, but I kept the same stoic facial expression. Bishop has no idea that he just basically threw me straight into the lion's den. Except this lion's hunger was not for food. Why the fuck couldn't he just be after food?

"Alright, I will. Havard, you go up first," I said stiffly, nodding towards the stairs. If I had to go up with him, I for damn sure wasn't going to have my back turned to him.

"Alright, Officer Kelby," he said, still keeping up with his little innocent act.

He headed for the stairs with me trailing behind him as we headed up to the second floor and then down to his cell. When we got there, I didn't know whether to keep him in front of me or put him behind me because either way, I knew he would be inside the cell with me and these cells are pretty small, so he would basically be on top of me, regardless. I was just hoping that he wouldn't be on me literally, though I knew that was futile.

It was only six feet by eight feet, so small was one way of putting it. The very back wall had a long, skinny rectangular window that replicated the one on the front cell door, but as mentioned, was longer. On the right wall was the tiny twin - if it was even that size - mattress with paper-thin sheets, a scratchy blanket, and a flat pillow that was elevated on a concrete slab that had a portion cut out under it to put shoes and clothes underneath and out of the way. At the foot of the bed was a tiny desk that was built into the wall out of concrete with some random items sitting atop, a single concrete shelf sat just above the desk with a concrete, cylindrical stool that was made built into the floor about three feet away from the desk. Immediately after the desk was the built-in combination steel sink and toilet, leaving the entire left wall bare.

"Where are the keys to my handcuffs located, Havard?" I asked as I walked into his cell. I heard the door close behind him as he came in as well, making me close my eyes as I forced myself not to sigh or groan. Damn if I didn't call it and know exactly what he planned on doing.

"Over here," Calder said, but I had my back to him so I didn't know where this 'over here' he was talking about was located.

"Over where Havard?" I asked impatiently, not wanting to turn around.

"Maybe if you turned around, you would see," he said, making me close my eyes and let out a silent sigh.

I know I'm going to end up regretting this, but here I am, turning around to face him to see him spinning my handcuff keys around his index finger, still wearing his normal smirk.

"You've had them with you the entire time, haven't you?" I said, not even trying to hide my annoyance. I should've fucking known.

"Maybe I have. Maybe I haven't," Calder shrugged, the smirk never having left his face since before we left Bishop, just widening more and more until his perfectly white, straight teeth were on full display. I noticed how sharp his canines looked.

"Hand them over," I demanded as I stretched my hand out to him which he clicked his tongue at with a shake of his head.

"No, no, no. That's not how this is going to work. I want to make an exchange," he said with an overexaggerated look of disappointment and a furrowed brow.

"I'm not exchanging anything with you. Just hand me my keys, which I know you took from me when you had me pinned yesterday, then I'll check your cell and leave," I said not in the mood for his shit - not like I ever am anyway, but even less so right now. My patience with him seemed to have been completely sapped after yesterday's...event. Just being this close to him was making me feel a little funny.

He glared at me and stood tall in an attempt to intimidate me, which was useless. I don't get intimidated or scared easily. Especially when I already know I can take him down and have done so on two separate occasions.

"No. We're doing things MY way," he growled out with a glare. It was very apparent that he was not used to being told no.

"Whatever helps you sleep at night, Havard. Now I won't ask again. Give. Me. My. Keys," I growled back lowly, shooting him my own glare right along with my words.

I watched as his eyes darkened and he bit his bottom lip, letting out a low grunt before he rushed me in two large strides, pushing me back and pinning me against the back wall of his cell, in much the same way as he did yesterday. It was like deja vu, and I didn't know how to feel about it.

"Fuck, you're so damn sexy, which is something I never expected to say to or about another guy in my life," he purred down at me, his entire tune changing in half a second.

"Back off, Havard," I snarled at him, making him hum in delight as he dropped his head down to my neck. He nudged the collar of my uniform shirt to the side where he began to softly bite at my skin making me shudder involuntarily and my cock go hard. Stupid fucking worthless piece of shit dick! Now is not the time!

"No. I get what I want. And what I want right now...is you," he spoke lowly, his voice husky and deep. I fought against the pleasurable shivers his tone evoked in me.

"Well, I don't want you," I said as I tried to push him off and away from me. He was quick to grab both of my hands, pinning them up alongside my head that was against the wall, leaving me no room to move or even attempt to escape.

Honestly, though, I doubt that my traitorous body would even move away from him anyway, not with the way my cock was beginning to swell inside of my already constricting pants. Dumb bitch.

"You can keep lying to yourself all you want, but I know what you want, and what you want is me," he breathed gruffly into my ear, sending goose-bumps rushing across the surface of my skin.

He pulled away slightly, making me let out a breath of relief only to suck it back in when he dropped his head and began to slowly drag the tip of his tongue from the base of my throat. From there, he then proceeded up my neck, along my jawline, and then over to run along the seam of my lips before he pressed his lips to mine. Unlike the rushed, rough kiss from yesterday, his lips moved slowly against mine, and against my mind's will, I followed his lead, letting him do as he pleased. He gently nibbled at my lips making me moan quietly and open my mouth up further to allow his tongue entry.

He slipped his tongue into my mouth, slowly brushing it against mine and setting my body on fire. His hands released my pinned ones slowly before moving lower down my sides until they had moved around my back and down lower where they settled on my ass which he didn't hesitate to give a firm squeeze. My eyes flew open at the action as my mind finally regained control of my body and what we were doing.

NO! I need to stop this now! I'm not gay!

I quickly brought up one of my hands, curling it into a fist and swinging it forward. My knuckles connected with the right side of his jaw making him bite down on my lip as he pulled away from me, clutching his jaw that was already starting to bruise lightly. I brought a hand up to my bottom lip to see that it, thankfully, wasn't bleeding.

"What the fuck, Darby?!" He growled at me, but this time in anger as his hand came up to cradle his smarting jaw.

"Stop fucking kissing me and touching me! I'm not fucking gay!" I yelled at him as I snatched my handcuff keys away from him that he had still been holding, and then shoulder-checked him as I pushed past him. I quickly checked his cell for any other contraband since I still had a job to do. But I purposely threw his blanket, pillow, and sheet across his bed in a childish form of retaliation before then moving on to looking under his bed.

"I'm not either!" He shouted back at me.

"Then why the fuck do you keep fucking kissing and touching me?!" I cried back in a mix of exasperation and confusion.

"I don't know! There's something about you that makes me want you! Besides, I've been here for five years. I'm pent up!" He continued to shout at me, throwing his hands up in the air.

I don't know why, but what he said struck a nerve in me. It both hurt and pissed me off that he was just planning on using me as his human sex toy whenever he wanted to. That shit is not happening! Not like it was going to anyway, though, since I have no interest in him or any other male.

"Yeah? Well either choose another guy or use your fucking hand! I'm not getting involved with you!" I said as I stood up after searching under his bed and coming up empty, then moving back to the safety of his cell door for an easy and quick exit.

"That's what you think!" Calder chortled back with a slight scoff.

"No, that's what I KNOW! I am a guard here, not an inmate fuck toy! And even if I was, I would never pick you! I don't like blondes," I shot at him.

I turned towards the door, about to open it to leave when he spoke. His words sent chills down my spine.

"You don't get it, do you? You don't have a choice here. I chose you, and you're going to give me what I want. The more you fight, the better it is because I like seeing you squirm. You're mine, and not just inside of these walls. You're mine when you walk out of here too," he said lowly, almost sounding sinister.

I hurried out of his cell and back down the stairs, quickly walking to a corner of the main area and leaning back against the wall. I let my normal blank expression slide into place, but I couldn't stop the rapid rise and fall of my chest. I just couldn't get it to ease up in the slightest, and I was pissed and worried by what he said.

I felt like I was trapped in some kind of sick, twisted game where Calder was the game master and I was just a piece he could do whatever he wanted with at any given moment in time.

The worst part of this entire fucked up situation is that until right now, I've never been one to be easily scared. And yet I was petrified because I didn't know how to control that fear to ease it.

I'm just as sick and twisted as he is. Maybe even worse because I would be completely pliant and willing to do it all just because it was him.

Walls Can't Keep Him Confined

I am pissed. No, fuck that. I am beyond pissed right now. I am fucking LIVID.

Not only did he deck me in the damn face, but he also refused me which never happens. I don't and I won't take no for an answer, and I made that very clear to him. And soon enough, he would learn that quite clearly.

I let out a loud, angry roar before turning and punching the wall that he had previously been pinned against where I let my tongue fuck his mouth. Where I had felt his ass and how fucking big and round it was. Where I started to imagine taking him up against the same wall, pounding mercilessly into his, no doubt, tight virgin ass.

I turned and walked to my cell door, throwing it open and walking out angrily. I stomped down the stairs, walking over to Bo and Gunnar who were playing cards at our usual table. As I approached, Bo looked up at me, eyebrows raised slightly.

"Based on the fact you look like a mad bull and that there's a bruise forming on your jaw, you were wrong," he said, fighting to stifle a laugh at my expense.

I shook my head, gritting my teeth as I sat down across from them, letting my nails dig into the skin on my palms as I let a snarl contort my features.

"No! I was fucking right but he keeps fighting it! We were good for about fifteen to twenty minutes before he punched me and started yelling at me!" I growled lowly.

"Yeah, because he's not interested, Calder! We tried to tell you that before you started on this...whatever it is, that you're going on about," Gunnar said as he sat his cards, face down, on the table before giving me his full attention.

"NO! No, I'm not wrong and I know it! You want to know how I know?" I said as I looked at them, my eyes alight with a fire I had never felt before.

"Not particularly, but I know you'll tell us anyway, so how do you know?" Bo sighed as he too dropped his cards, face down, on the table before raising his arm to rest his elbow on the table, cradling his face in his propped-up hand.

"Because he told me that he wasn't an inmate fuck toy, and if he was, he wouldn't pick me because he's not into blondes," I said with a confident smirk.

Bo and Gunnar looked at each other in disbelief before they looked at me and then spoke at the same time.

"Yes, because he's. Not. Interested!" They exclaimed, acting as if they were talking to a child, which I sure as hell was not. I rolled my eyes at them since they weren't understanding a damn thing I was saying.

"Whatever. It doesn't matter anyway because he's mine," I said with a possessive edge to my words.

They looked at me like I was crazy, and hell, maybe I was. But I wasn't fucking around when it came to Darby.

"Wait...yours?! Didn't we just talk about this not being a serious thing? That this was just for FUN?!" Gunnar said, looking even more floored than he was before, and even slightly pissed.

"It was supposed to just be for fun, but that was back before he thought he'd have a choice in the matter. But he fucked up now. I have a few calls to make, I'll be back," I said as I stood up, dropping the conversation as a plan began to formulate in my mind.

"Calls? Calls to who?" Bo questioned suspiciously.

"A few guys at home. I want a constant detail on him from now on," I said as I walked to the phones, Bo and Gunnar following along behind me.

"Aren't you being a little, uh, I don't know...CRAZY?!" Gunnar exclaimed.

"No, if anything he is. I want him to realize that his ass is mine!" I seethed, getting worked up all over again.

A phone opened up just as I reached the long wall of phones available for inmate use, and I immediately took it, beginning to make my calls.

Was he going to be pissed at me for what I was doing? Probably. Did I care? Nope, not one bit. Why? Because he was going to learn the hard way what my claim on him meant.

- Darby's POV -

It's now the day after Calder had pinned me to his cell wall and we had made out before I punched him. Thankfully, both today and tomorrow are my two days off which means that I get a two-day break from Calder and his bullshit. Thank God.

And because I have these two, full days off, I was going to look at some TVs and ovens before coming home to get ready for a club night with Grant where I hoped to find someone to occupy my mind, time, and hopefully my dick too, for the night.

I was currently on my way to a warehouse - no, it wasn't a sketchy place, I had already made sure of that - where used appliances and electronics were sold. W was hoping to find some decently priced ovens and TVs that I could buy since I was going crazy without either, especially a TV. My place was too damn quiet without one, and that meant that my mind was constantly occupied by unwanted thoughts of a certain blonde jackass.

I parked in a space in front of the large, cream-colored concrete building, then got out of my car, and headed into the store. As I entered, I decided to first look at the oven options they had in store since that is what I caught sight of first.

The only cheaper ones they had looked like someone had either dropped or beaten them to death with a sledgehammer, so it was a no-go on ovens from here. If I got one from here it probably wouldn't even work based on how shitty they looked. Now on to the next thing: a TV.

As I walked towards the TVs, I felt like I was being followed, or at least watched by someone. I turned slightly, pretending to be interested in a microwave as I glanced up and around me, using the reflection on the door of the microwave to see a guy attempting to discreetly watch me as he texted on his phone. He was awful at trying to not be detected if that was even what he was attempting to do.

I continued to browse but I kept alert to confirm that he was, indeed, following me. Which, as I already knew, he was since he sucked at following me.

Regardless, I continued on with my task as I went over to the TVs and looked at their selection. It was just as shitty as their ovens. Realizing that this place was a bust, I turned and headed out of the warehouse where I planned on confronting my follower when he would no doubt follow me out.

I stepped out of the warehouse and walked down the front of it before ducking around the side of the building, stopping just around the corner and pressing as close to the side of the building as possible so that I wouldn't be seen. Something that he should have been doing inside earlier if he knew how to do his job properly.

Suddenly the guy came hurrying around the corner, looking the tiniest bit frantic at having thought he'd lost me. Little did he know that I was onto him, and waiting for this precise moment.

I quickly wrapped my arm around his throat as I spun him around pressing him against the side of the building, keeping my arm locked around his neck firmly as he struggled. I grabbed his other arm, pulling it up painfully against his back. If I were to add just the slightest bit more pressure, I would surely snap his shoulder, or at the very least pop the joint out of place. But that was only if I decided not to be nice and applied too much additional pressure. The way he would respond to my questions would determine his shoulder's fate.

"AHH! FUCK, LET ME GO, DUDE!" The guy wailed in pain and what seemed like fear as well. What a little chicken shit, he can't even handle a little bit of pain or conceal his emotions like a good stalker would do. Pathetic.

"No. Why the fuck are you following me?!" I demanded of him. He shook his head back and forth in the negatory so fast that it was almost comical to watch.

"I'm not, dude! I swear to you I'm not!" He denied it desperately, looking even more terrified. Though he was denying it, it was clear to see he was lying and really was. But then again, I had way been onto him, so it was no use in denying it anyway.

"I smell bullshit. Why are you following me? Answer me!" I growled as I added the tiniest bit more pressure to his arm making him cry out in pain before he started to sing like a bird.

"AHH! OKAY OKAY! MY BOSS! MY BOSS SENT ME TO FOLLOW YOU!" He shrieked out shrilly. I had never heard a guy's voice reach that high a pitch before.

"Boss?! Who's your boss?!" I pressed him, teasing him by adding varying degrees of pressure on his arm, mainly toying with his pressure points without truly adding any additional pressure to his shoulder. All I had to do was play with his mind a little, and he was easy to open up.

"AHH! C-CALDER HAVARD!" He squirmed, trying to break my iron grip, but I fully released him with a growl. I paced back and forth angrily at this new tidbit of information.

"I can't believe that mother fucker!" I boomed, absolutely pissed that he now had me being followed by his fucking lackeys or whatever they were to him.

A rapid and dull repeated thudding sound drifted to my ears making me look to see the guy typing away on his phone, fingers flying across the on-screen keyboard.

"Are you texting him right now?!" I cried out in rage.

"Yes, I have to tell him! Fuck man, you probably just got me killed for having caught me!" He said, pausing in his typing to look at me with wide, terrified hazel eyes. They even looked a little misty, making me feel a little bad for him but my rage was easily trumping that down.

"Then don't be so fucking obvious!" I shouted at him like the imbecile he was.

My phone ringing loudly in my back pocket stopped me from tearing into him more as I pulled it out to see an unknown number. Normally, I wouldn't answer but I decided to this time, a sinking feeling filling the pit of my stomach as I did so.

"Hello? Who is this?" I questioned down the line.

"Your favorite inmate, of course."

Why this mother fucker...

A Not-So-Good Time

"Hello? Who is this?" I questioned down the line.

"Your favorite inmate, of course," came the annoying, deep husky voice that seemed to haunt me anymore.

"You aren't," I spat back, glaring hard at the concrete wall of the warehouse in front of me, wishing it was his face so he could see it. Then quickly taking it back knowing that he would just start kissing me or something to that effect since that was apparently his thing.

"Ouch, Darby. I'm wounded," he said, feigning hurt which only served to further annoy me as I rolled my eyes.

"Oh well. Now, how the hell did you get my cell phone number?" I demanded.

"I've got connections," he said coyly making me want to reach through the phone and strangle his cryptic ass.

"Is that going to be your answer for how you got this cell phone since I know it's not one that is offered in the Penitentiary?" I shot back at him, feeling even more irritated.

"Yes, it is," he said, a smirk in his voice before his tone turned condescending. "Now, why are you attacking a member of my Mafia?"

"Um, gee let me see...because the fucker is following me and I know that you had him do it! All I want to know is why the fuck you're having me followed?" I growled, clenching my phone tighter in my hand as I held it up to my ear, eager to hear whatever bullshit would next be spewed.

"It's simple really. I want to know where you go and who you're with at all times."

He said it so casually like he didn't just admit to having someone fucking tailing me constantly now. What. The. Fuck.

"Why, though?! Why can't you just leave me alone?!" I cried out exasperatedly. I was feeling drained from talking to him, even if it hadn't even been five minutes on the phone with him yet.

He let out a low, dark, and almost sinister chuckle that had goosebumps covering my skin within seconds. I'm undecided on whether they were good or bad ones, and quite frankly, I don't even want to know.

"I told you before, Darby. You are mine and no one else can have you! I won't let them!" He rumbled out.

"That's not something you can decide. You need to get over your obsession with me. I have to go, now. I'm going out tonight with a friend where I'm going to fuck a couple of bitches. And there's not a damn thing you can do about it!" I growled lowly into the phone before hanging up just before he could respond. I deliberately relayed my intentions for tonight, all in an effort to piss him off since that is what he was doing to me. I'm not going to let myself get sucked into his sick game any more than I already am. I was going to give him a little taste of his own medicine if you will.

I looked up at the guy who had been tailing me all day who still looked scared shitless. Poor guy.

"What's your name?" I asked him in an effort to distract us both from what had just occurred.

"Sven Jacubsen," he answered without hesitation.

"Well Sven, consider my next words as a warning. I don't want you following me. I want you to leave me alone and stop texting him shit about me!" I snapped at him with a glare.

"I'm sorry but I can't do that. I take my orders from my boss, not you," he replied, but I could see the slightest hint of remorse in his eyes. But that didn't stop my rage.

I growled angrily before turning and running to my car, hopping in and quickly driving off. As I headed back to my place, I made sure to check that I wasn't being followed, even going a bunch of crazy ways just to be sure. Thankfully, I wasn't.

I pulled into the parking lot of my apartment complex and parked in my usual spot, jumping out and hurrying inside. I still had about an hour before I needed to get ready so I decided to just lay in my bed for that time, and just decompress a little.

After the hour, I got up, took a shower, and then got dressed in a loose-fitting white tee, a navy blue collared button down with ivory-colored buttons and a chest pocket on either side, paired with grey wool trousers, and black Wall Street Driving Shoes with a silver buckle across the top. I even gave my hair a quick styling that was just me wetting my fingers with water from the sink, and running them through the front of my hair, pushing it to the right as I went for a kind of wind-swept look. Now that I was ready for the night, I headed downstairs and got into my awaiting Uber that I'd sent for ahead of time, and then headed to the same club I'd gone with Grant to before I started work at the Penitentiary.

Upon arriving, I got out of my Uber and walked straight into the club since I hadn't seen Grant waiting outside for me anywhere. As I walked up to the bar, I saw him flirting with a dark-headed girl which was funny since he tended to avoid them.

As I reached him, I gave his arm a nudge to signal to him that I'd arrived without butting into his little flirt-fest. He instantly paused his talking to turn around and grin at me.

"Darby, hey man! It's been a while!" He greeted me excitedly making me chuckle and nod at him.

"Yeah, it really has been! Work has been crazy! Like you wouldn't believe how crazy it is!" I said with a shake of my head, not wanting to get into the details of the shit I was going through. Crazy didn't even begin to describe it.

"You work at Terminus Penitentiary, so of course, it is!" He shot back, looking at me the way he had first done when I told him about my new job.

I mean, he's not wrong, but he doesn't know the true extent of the crazy that I have to deal with because of a particular Nordic Mafia leader. The fucking asshole.

"So, who's your friend?" I asked, changing the subject, as I nodded in the direction of the girl who was eyeing the both of us up now, her teeth lightly pressing against her bottom lip as she attempted to give us a sultry grin.

Normally I'd be getting hard at the beautiful sight, but right now I wasn't and it was pissing me the hell off. But I forced myself to shrug it off, putting my dick's inactivity off to being tired from being fucked up around the blonde asshole.

"Some girl I just met. Looks like my fuck for the night," he muttered quietly to me while I chuckled at him.

"I thought you preferred blondes?" I questioned, to which he gave a shrug in response with a small grin.

"I figured I'd give brunettes a chance," he said nonchalantly, making me arch a brow. He had always sworn them off. Saying their hair looked dirty or something stupid like that, but whatever.

"Okay then," I said, thinking it was going to be left at that.

"Hey, you should give blondes a try then since I'm giving brunettes a try," he suggested, giving my shoulder a nudge like I'd given him when I first got here, as well as wiggling his eyebrows at me.

My body tensed as my mind immediately conjured up an image of a smirking Calder towering over me as I was pressed up against a wall. I mentally shook my head as I clenched my hands into fists.

"Yeah, uh, um, I'll have to think about it," I said stiffly, not wanting to do that at all.

"Just saying, don't knock it til you've tried it," he winked at me.

I just nodded, thinking that I would be trying more than just a blonde if I gave in as he said, but the thought had my stomach twisting uneasily making me flag down a bartender who I asked for a whiskey sour.

"I'm going to go find myself a good fuck for the night because God knows I need it," I said after nodding my thanks to the bartender who slid my drink over to me.

"Alright. I think I might head out with this girl now. Sorry, I know we came to hang out together but you know-" he started, looking a little guilty, but I cut him off.

"It's fine, Grant. Just go, I'll be fine," I waved him off, having expected nothing less from him. This was a regular occurrence when we went out together most of the time, so I wasn't too worried about being left alone, plus I could easily hold my own if need be.

"Sweet, you're the best, man. Bye," he grinned, and then off he went with the girl he had been chatting with, leaving me to drink alone. As usual. While sipping on my drink, my eyes scanned the crowded club, looking for someone, anyone that made my dick twitch. Yet no matter which type of girl I looked at, I felt nothing, so I decided to just pick some girl at random.

I necked back my drink before making my way over to some girl who I had noticed eyeing me the entire time I had been at the bar. Just like the last time I was here and was with a girl over a month ago, I pushed her against the wall, not saying a word to her as our lips crashed together. I was here for one thing, and one thing only so pleasantries were off of the table.

As I kissed her, I couldn't help but think that this was all wrong. Her lips were too soft and sticky from what felt like a mix of chapstick and lip gloss making me want to gag. Even after I dropped my pants and boxers, put on a condom, and pushed inside of her after pulling her thong down to her thighs from under her skirt, I felt nothing at all and my cock stayed soft the entire time. It also felt disgusting and had me feeling a bit nauseous too.

Either she didn't notice or she didn't care, as she continued to moan loudly without a care in the world. Such a desperate bitch. As soon as she came, I pulled out, pulled off the condom, tossed it to the side, pulled up my pants and boxers, and then walked off angrily.

As I angrily walked to the exit of the club I saw him again. Sven. The guy Calder had hired to follow me. He was looking from me to his phone, not even caring that I could see him as his fingers were once again tapping rapidly on his phone screen.

Tonight night was a bust, especially since I didn't get to. All I wanted was to go home and get drunk on my couch in the dark as I tried to figure out how I got to where I was now: unsatisfied and confused.

So, that's exactly what I did.

Slip of the Tongue

BANG! BANG! BANG!

"Darby! Darby where the fuck are you?! I know you're here! I saw your car in the parking lot!"

BANG! BANG! BANG!

I jerked up and looked around to see that I had passed out on my couch, three empty bottles of liquor around me and an almost empty fourth bottle still tightly clutched in my left hand.

It took me a moment to remember that I had ended up stopping off at a liquor store on my way home and then drinking away my sorrows and anger on my couch before passing out at some time during the night.

Sorrows because my damn dick no longer worked. And anger because it was all fucking Calder's fault that my dick decided that it only wanted to get hard for him.

"DARBY! ANSWER THE FUCKING DOOR OR I'M BREAKING THE BITCH DOWN!" Grant's voice came screaming throughout my tiny apartment. His loud voice echoed around in my head painfully making me recall that someone was beating the hell out of my front door which had roused me from my sleep in the first place. That someone obviously being Grant.

I stood slowly, swaying some as I winced. The pulsing pain increased to almost a stabbing sensation in my head as I stumbled to my front door, throwing it open to get him to stop.

"About damn time that- What the fuck happened to you?!" Grant shouted out as he looked at me with his eyes nearly popping out of his head.

"For fucks sake, Grant, stop yelling!" I growled at him before wincing at the sound of my own loud voice. Everything was too fucking loud. Why couldn't I have been gifted the sweet sound of silence when I woke up?

"Shit, how much did you drink at the club after I left?" He asked as he walked passed me and into my apartment, looking me up and down as he came in.

"Not a damn thing. I stayed for maybe twenty more minutes and then left. I went to a liquor store afterward, bought some bottles, came home, and then drank them all by myself," I grumbled quietly as I nodded over to my couch which was still littered with liquor bottles. He turned and upon seeing the mess, let out a low whistle.

"Damn, that's kind of depressing. What's up with you? Not find any good pussy again last night?" Grant snickered to himself, thinking that he was just poking fun at me.

"You could say that," I said as I walked passed him and back over to my couch. I began picking up all of my empty liquor bottles and the nearly-empty one, before walking around the tiny bartop of my kitchen, and throwing them in my trash can.

"What's going on with you? Ever since you first started at that Penitentiary, you've changed," Grant questioned me, his gaze burning holes into me as he scrutinized me.

"Trust me, I know. And you wouldn't even understand if I tried to explain the cause of it," I muttered as I leaned down and rested my head on my kitchen counter. My head was pounding from the mix of alcohol and my mind spinning thought of Calder around in it nonstop.

"Why don't you try and explain it so I can be the judge of that?!" Grant snapped at me in irritation.

My head popped up from my arms as I looked at him with semi-wide eyes. I hadn't expected him to have heard me, so knowing that he did was making me start to panic slightly, but I was trying not to let it show too much.

"It's not important. Just ignore what I said," I said quickly with a slight shrug, moving to walk passed him. But he grabbed my shoulder and pulled me to a stop, turning me back around to face him.

"No! Talk to me, Darby! We've been best friends for years and we have always been close but ever since you got this new job, you don't talk to me as much, and when you do, I can tell that something's bothering you! But whenever I ask you about it, you brush me off!" Grant snapped at me with a slight glare that instantly had my hackles raised in defense.

"Grant, I'm fucking fine! Don't worry about-" I started, just wanting him to drop the subject, but he was as persistent as always as he cut me off.

"There! Right here is a perfect example of you just brushing me off!" He yelled at me.

"Yeah because I'm not ready to talk about it and I don't know if I ever will be!" I yelled right back at him, panting slightly from how upset I had become.

"And why not?! What is so bad that you can't even tell me, your best friend, what's going on?!" Grant shouted even louder.

And then, because I was feeling pissed and overwhelmed, I opened my big mouth and told him what I'd been battling inside of me ever since Calder first pressed his fucking intoxicating lips to mine.

"Because one of the fucking inmates kissed me and I liked it! Now I can't fucking get him out of my head, and I think I'm gay!"

He went dead silent for a moment as his mouth dropped open in surprise, and his eyes widened before he took several shocking steps away from me.

"What did you just say?" He asked lowly.

I took a step toward him, wanting to try and explain a little better.

"Grant I-"

"NO! Get back and just...and just stay the fuck away from me!" He spat out.

I stopped in my tracks as it was now my turn to look at him in shock and disbelief.

"Grant you can't be serious right now! Are you really pissed over the fact that I MIGHT be gay?!" I asked, completely dumbfounded by his sudden change in behavior around me.

"No, I'm not pissed, I'm fucking weirded out and...and disgusted! You've always liked girls, you've always liked pussy! And now, suddenly, you like dick?! That shit is not right! And you said it's an inmate! Darby that's even worse! I knew that if you started working there, it would fuck you up and I was right!" He snarled at me, looking at me like I was a piece of gum stuck to the bottom of his shoe.

I couldn't believe that someone I thought was my best friend, who I thought I knew, was so awful and cruel!

"Get out, Grant. GET THE FUCK OUT AND DON'T COME BACK! EVER!" I screamed at him to which he growled back at me in his own rage before turning around and leaving my apartment, slamming the door on the way out.

I stood there still for a moment, still panting from my own anger, letting it build up inside of me. When I couldn't take it any longer, I let out a loud, angry scream.

The only person who I was ever close to just left me all because there's a possibility that I'm gay and I've never felt more alone in all of my life than I do right now.

Bubbling Over

I slept like shit last night, hell, I'm not even sure if I even fell asleep. I tossed and turned all night, still feeling the loss of the only person who I thought I could depend on. But it turns out he's like everyone else I've ever known: undependable.

Aside from the shit storm that was currently happening in my life, I did have a small silver lining as I headed to work the following day: I had bought some new pants for my uniform. Currently, that was the only positive thing I had going for me right now.

I pulled into a spot in the Penitentiary parking lot and got out, reaching over to grab my water bottle and granola bar that weren't there in their normal spot in the passenger seat.

I had forgotten them back at my apartment. I remember setting them on the counter after I got them out and ready to take with me, but I never went back for them after I had finished getting dressed, instead, I had walked out of the door, still thinking about the sting of betrayal that sat heavy in my chest.

I repeatedly punched my steering wheel angrily as I felt tears well in my eyes as the stress and frustration I had bottled in me threatened to burst free, but I refused to let a single tear fall. I took in a few long deep breaths to calm myself before finally getting out of my car and heading inside, feeling completely numb.

If it weren't for the fact that I still needed money for a new TV and oven, I would have just called out sick. But I can't, I need money and I also need to be occupied enough that I don't recall all of my troubles. It would be a great distraction.

I eventually made it back to the unit after scanning my badge, immediately heading to the office where I scanned my badge again and walked inside to throw my car keys and phone in my locker. After I closed it, I rested my head against the door, again slowly trying to take in a few breaths and push back my feeling of complete and utter despair and loneliness.

I heard the door open followed by loud chatter and laughter, which quickly prompted me to stand up straight and put on my normal emotionless face.

Time to get to work.

- Calder's POV -

I couldn't wait for Darby to get in so that I could pin him to a wall and kiss the fuck out of him again and then hear him yell at me for kissing him. It was so damn refreshing, and I found it sexy as hell.

I don't know what it is about him, but he's the only person who's ever hit or yelled at me and lived. But I fucking love it when he does it, and it just makes me want him more, which is quite apparent.

I was staring at the clock hanging in the front of the unit, watching the time tick by. I was thrilled when it was finally time for shift change and for him to come in after his weekend off. My eyes went to the door, seeing him walking in as he always did. Disappointment filled me when I noticed that he no longer had those tight pants, but I was also a little happy because that meant that the other guys wouldn't eye him up as much anymore.

But as I watched him, I noticed that there was something wrong with him. Not in a bad way, like he was sick or hurt. But he looked upset with his head hung low, his body slumped forward. He looked like he was carrying the weight of the world on his shoulders. I was instantly concerned, wanting to know what had caused such a reaction from him and who I had to kill for hurting him.

"Your guard didn't look like he was doing too hot, Calder," Gunnar said, but my eyes remained locked on Darby as he hurried into the guard's office area.

"Yeah I know," I said quietly, my eyes locked on the door to the guards' room.

"It's probably your fault," Bo said, a smirk easily decipherable in his voice.

At that, I snapped my head around and glared at him angrily. I would never do a single thing to make him look like that. Never.

"Watch it, Bo! I haven't done anything wrong!" I snarled at him, unable to stop my lip from raising up to show my teeth.

He immediately threw his hands up in the air, looking a bit uneasy at my sudden show of aggression.

"Hey, I was just screwing with you, man! Just take a breath and relax!" Bo attempted to placate me.

I clenched my fists as I looked back to the guard's office door, but he had yet to exit it making me even more agitated.

"I can't. He's upset and I want to know why," I grunted, clenching my hands into fists.

"Maybe you should take a step back and just give him some time," Gunnar suggested.

"No! Whether he admits it or not, he wants and needs me!" I refused instantly, feeling my possessiveness for him rise.

"Really? Because right now it kind of seems like you want and need him more than he needs or wants you," Bo said with a shrug.

I locked my jaw, ignoring his comment as I watched the other guards for the night shift come into the unit and then the guards' area. Moments later, out walked Darby, his face even more stony than usual which just made me worry even more about what was going on with him.

"Dude, stop staring and frowning at him," Gunnar hissed at me.

"I need to talk to him," I said as I stood up.

"Wait, what?" Bo asked, looking startled.

"Where are you going?" Gunnar asked.

"Back hallway. The cameras are down. Go tell him I'm fighting someone or I'm about to, or just...anything. Just get him to come back there," I said, turning to give them stern looks.

"Is that really a good idea?" Bo asked unsurely.

"Probably not, but you two agreed to help me so you're going to. Now tell him," I said stiffly.

And with that I left, walking to the back hallway where I leaned against the wall, waiting for him to come back here. I knew he would come, it was just a matter of how soon he would get back here.

- Darby's POV -

I've been leaning against the wall, watching to make sure everything is in order. I had been here for all of maybe fifteen minutes into my shift when both of Calder's buddies came running up to me.

"Kelby! We need your help!" The tattoo-sleeve-covered one, Gunnar, called out.

"If it has to do with Havard, go get another guard," I dismissed them immediately. I didn't want to have to deal with jack shit that pertained to him.

"But he's got another inmate in the back hallway! He's pissed at him!" The ditzier, jokester one, Bo, cried out in a panic.

A deep scowl covered my face at that. Of course, he was going to cause a fight, and quite possibly another riot by killing a guy. I didn't want to deal with all of that shit, so I pushed off of the wall to go deal with him.

I pushed passed them and quickly headed down the back hallway, wanting to get there and end whatever he was starting so I could resume my post and ignore him. The moment I turned the corner to the back hallway, I stopped. Calder was just casually leaning against the wall, all by himself, doing nothing wrong. This was a fucking setup.

I shook my head in irritation and turned around to quickly leave, throwing a few words over my shoulder at him.

"No. I'm not in the mood for your shit today, Calder. Just no."

I had almost made it fully back around the corner when his hand caught my wrist and spun me back around to face him, quickly pushing me into his preferred position with me pressed against the wall. He had to have a fucking obsession with keeping me pinned between himself and walls.

"I don't care if you are in the mood for my 'shit' or not. I can tell something is bothering you," he said, a stern edge to his voice.

"Yeah, so what?" I said, my voice a little snappy but I didn't care. He deserved it for all the shit he's put me through.

"Talk to me, Darby. Tell me what's wrong," Calder said, though I could hear that he didn't intend it to be a request. It was a demand.

I let out a bitter laugh as I tilted my head back to rest it against the wall. He was so much taller than me that I was just looking up at him fully now.

"What isn't wrong anymore?! Everything in my life is wrong and it's all fucking thanks to you!" I snapped at him bitterly.

He took a surprised, half-step back before pressing even closer to me, placing his forehead up against mine as he growled lowly.

"Me?! How the fuck is whatever is going on with you MY fault?!"

"Because ever since you fucking kissed me you fucked up my head and broke my dick!" I growled at him, my earlier anger surging to the forefront yet again.

His eyebrows shot up in surprise, the anger melting off of his face and quickly morphing into a smirk as he leaned back some and looked down at my cock that was immediately hardening under his gaze.

Again, my dick is a traitorous fucker.

"Oh yeah? How'd I break your dick? I mean, I haven't even had the chance to touch it yet," Calder asked, his voice even lower and deeper, making me fight to hold back a pitiful moan.

Fuck me and my big mouth that has decided to spill all of my thoughts and problems. I just love bringing more trouble to myself.

"I can't get fucking hard anymore," I grunted as I moved my face to the side in an attempt to avoid his gaze and protect my lips from his. I knew that eventually he would try and kiss me, especially with the position we were in.

"Really? Because from what I just saw, you are definitely hard," he said, pressing his left leg to my right thigh, inches away from my hardened cock.

For the first time in my entire life, I felt heat rushing to my cheeks out of embarrassment as I continued to speak, keeping my voice low.

"You're the only one who can make me hard."

Out of the corner of my eye, I saw him smirking cockily at me. He lifted his hand up to gently grab ahold of my chin and turn my face back around to look at him.

"Good, and it's going to stay that way too because like I've been telling you: You. Are. Mine. You say that your dick can only get hard for me, yet you stuck it in some other bitch on Saturday. It's mine and no one else gets it. Only me," he growled seductively with a searing heat that had tingles spreading across my body.

But I pushed that all away as I looked at him in confusion for having known about that when he was here at the Penitentiary.

"How the fuck did you kno-" I stopped as I remembered my fucking follower. It was courtesy of him that Calder knew. "Fucking Sven told you. Of course, the nosy fucker did," I growled angrily which just had him pushing into me even further.

"He's doing what I told him to do, so be pissed off at me all you want," Calder said with a cocky shrug.

I shoved him off of me, moving quickly as I pinned him, face-first, into the wall. I grabbed both of his arms and pulled them behind his back before grabbing my cuffs and locking them around his wrists.

"Hey! What the fuck did you cuff me for?!" Calder grunted at me.

"Because I can," I growled as I pulled him off of the wall, beginning to push him forward to start walking.

"But I didn't do anything wrong!" He huffed out angrily.

"Really? You have one of your guys following me, you keep pinning me to walls and kissing me-" I began to list.

"I haven't gotten my kiss today yet, so that will be happening soon," he interjected smugly but I ignored him and carried on speaking.

"-and you have a cellphone somewhere that someone gave you. So I'm going to be finding that, and confiscating it."

"Okay, but I'll just get another one," he said, and I could hear the smirk in his voice which just further irritated me.

We finally made it back to the main area and headed straight to the stairs to head up to the second floor. The moment we hit the top of the stairs to the second floor, both of his friends, Bo and Gunnar, stood there looking highly amused.

"So based on the fact that you're cuffed by him again, things didn't go well I assume?" Gunnar teased with an arched brow.

"I got the information I wanted from him, and he got pissy again," Calder said sounding happy which made me scowl at him as I lifted my hand up and pushed his head forward making him growl.

"Move it. To your cell. I need to find that phone," I told him sternly making him let out a low groan.

"Fuck, I love it when you get all pissy and rough with me! It gets me so fucking horny!" He said lustfully, momentarily shocking me.

Both Bo and Gunnar looked between us in shock and I quickly pushed him forward, heading straight for his cell. Once we got to his cell I opened the door and walked in, knowing that he had already escaped the cuffs the moment that I had let go of his hands.

That was confirmed a few seconds later when I heard his cell door shut behind me and then heard the cuffs hit his small table to the side of us as he tossed them away. I heard him coming closer to me as I checked under his mattress for the phone he has that he used to call me with over the weekend.

"Back it up, Havard," I said without pausing in my search

"Hmm, let me think about it..." He said, pretending to consider my request. But even as he did, I felt him walk up behind me, placing both of his hands on either side of my waist as he pressed his solid cock to my ass making me gasp in shock. "How about no."

No Regrets

My eyes were wide as I stared down at his bed as I felt him pressing his erection into my ass.

I was frozen in shock yet I was also enjoying the feeling of having his cock pressed up against me. I knew he could tell just how much based on the fact that I had yet to move away from him and that I wasn't making any effort to do so, either.

"Fuck! I have never wanted someone so bad in my life until you came around!" He groaned out lowly.

"Not my fault," I said stiffly as I grabbed the edge of his bed tightly and he started to slowly move his erection against my ass, driving me mad.

But I remained motionless, not knowing what to do or what to expect from him. I also didn't want to give him any hint that what he was doing was okay, not wanting to further encourage him.

"Oh, yes it is! You have the best ass I've ever seen, and damn good lips that I want all the time, but you like to always fight and test me. Something that no one has ever dared to do without ending up dead. And yet, here you are, doing it to me every single day. You've punched me and brought me down to my knees, twice, and I can't help but to want more. Want YOU more," he growled.

"I'm not letting you fuck me in the ass," I said quickly, even though I couldn't help but clench my ass at the thought. It was taking just about everything I had in me to stop me from pushing my ass further back against his solid erection. To feel more of him.

"Maybe right now you won't, but I know that someday soon you will. But for now, I will just have to make do with kissing you," he sighed dramatically.

"And if I don't want you to?" I asked, hearing him let out a low, deep chuckle before he flipped me around in one fluid motion. He had my back pressed to his bed as he climbed up over the top of me to stare down at me hungrily.

"That's funny because I know that you want me to. Otherwise, you wouldn't be as hard as you are for me right now."

He dropped his head down to gently nudge at my neck with his nose before he began to pepper light kisses on my neck, lightly nibbling on my skin with each drag of his lips.

"Hnnngh! C-Calder!" I moaned at the odd tickling sensation.

"Mmm. That's the first time you've said my actual first name. You should say it more," he purred as he kissed all up and down my neck, making me tremble with desire. The desire for his lips to be on mine.

"Calder, fucking kiss me dammit!" I snapped at him, unable to hold myself back any longer. He was just too damn tempting, almost addicting in the way he moved.

"See? I told you that you would be begging me to kiss you in no time," he teased as he pulled his head back, lips leaving my neck as he smirked down at me sultrily.

"Just shut the fuck up and kiss me."

"Gladly, Darby," he said right before he dropped his head down, finally connecting our lips causing stars to dot my vision.

I shut my eyes to try and clear my vision, but only ended up falling further into the kiss and the pleasure it gave me. I was tired of denying the truth: I was attracted to an inmate. To the leader of a Mafia, the Nordic Mafia to be precise. And there wasn't a single thing that I could do to fight those feelings.

His lips started off moving slowly against mine, but it wasn't long until he was kissing me even harder than before making my cock grow and pulse with desire that I was just barely supressing, not wanting to go much further than this. At least not today.

I moaned happily as I let my hands move up to his surprisingly soft hair which felt so good in between my fingers and had me tugging on it in order to feel more of its silkiness.

He dropped his hips from where they had been hovering over mine, as he began to grind his hardened cock against mine, pulling more moans out of me with each push and pull of his hips against mine.

Suddenly, a few rapid, almost urgent knocks were being banged on his cell door. I freaked out as I tried to get out from under him, but he kept me pinned down to the bed as he turned around to face the door, anger contorting his features in an instant.

"WHAT?!" He snarled as the door opened seconds later. It was Bo and Gunnar who were sticking their heads in, smirking as they saw me pinned underneath Calder.

"Are we interrupting something?" Gunnar asked with a smirk.

"Yes! Now what do you two want?!" Calder spat out angrily at the two.

"It's not us, it's Bishop. He's looking for Darby since he hasn't seen him in a while," Bo explained.

"Stupid ass fucker is ruining my fun!" Calder huffed angrily. I began to push more urgently against his chest, trying to get the heavy fucker off of me so I could get back out on the floor.

"Get off of me, Calder! I need to go before he finds out!" I hissed at him.

"It's fine. He won't find out so stop worrying so damn much," he said as he finally got up off of me, allowing me to hurry to my feet. I quickly righted my uniform so it didn't look like I had just been having a makeout session, the opposite of what I should have been doing, which was working.

"That's easy for you to say, you're not supposed to be working right now like I am. I need this job to be able to afford shit for myself," I said as I went to walk out of his cell, but yet again, he caught me by my wrist, making me stop to look at him. "What now? I have to go."

"You can go after I get another kiss," he said with a smirk.

"We were just making out, you got your kiss then," I shot back at him, tired of him and his bullshit.

But he was insistent as he gave a tug on my arm, forcing me to stumble closer to him so that we were now pressed chest to chest.

"Well, I want another one. And I'm going to get another one," he said as he leaned in towards me.

Even though I wanted to give in to him and kiss him again, I knew that if we did, I would end up pinned somewhere in this cell again and he wouldn't let me go this time. So, I dodged his approaching lips, ducking as I managed to pull my hand out of his grasp before I hurried away from him. I stopped for only a second to grab my handcuffs before hurrying out of his cell, smirking to myself as I heard him let out a loud, annoyed growl at my escape.

I walked slowly down the stairs so as to not raise suspicion, and began to make my rounds around the main area as I always did, clearing my face of any emotion like normal.

"Darby!"

I stopped, turning to look behind me to see Bishop coming up to me with a kind of mystified look on his face.

"Yeah, Bishop?" I asked cooly.

"Where the fuck have you been? I haven't seen you for almost half an hour!" He asked.

"I had to head to the back hallway earlier since there was talk of a possible fight. After that I headed up to the second floor to make sure everything was in order up there, just in case any of the inmates were planning something somewhere up there," I said.

I shouldn't be this good at lying but I am thanks to Calder.

"Okay then," he said as he turned to look at the inmates that were scattered throughout the main area, the majority of them seated at the tables playing cards or just talking to each other.

As we watched over the inmates, my eyes locked on Calder who was now downstairs and seated at his normal table with Bo and Gunnar who were chuckling at him as he sulked. When he noticed me looking at him, he glared at me and I had to bite the inside of my cheek to keep from laughing at him. Apparently, he still wasn't very happy with me for not kissing him before I left his cell earlier.

"Calder Havard really isn't a fan of yours, is he?" Bishop said as he chuckled when he saw the glare Calder was giving me. If he only knew how much of a fan he is of mine, he would probably fire me and shit himself, not necessarily in that order.

"Yeah, it seems that way," I said simply.

"I'm honestly surprised that he hasn't tried to attack you or something," Bishop added. Again, if he only knew that he had attacked me, multiple times, in a way that was the complete opposite way that he's thinking, he would fire me and shit himself.

"Kind of seems like he's all bark and no bite. Like a pussy cat," I shrugged.

"You two talking shit over here Kelby and Bishop?"

I turned my head around to see Calder standing a few feet away from us, arms crossed and brow raised with an otherwise straight face. But I could see in his eyes that he wanted nothing more than to pin me to the wall that was a foot or two behind me. I swear he has some kind of fetish with doing that to me.

"Maybe, but I'm not sure how that is any concern of yours though," I said with a raised brow of my own, still fighting to conceal an amused smirk.

"Watch it, Kelby," he growled as he took a few steps forward toward me, but I wasn't threatened or intimidated by him in the least.

"Alright, that's enough, Calder. Back it up," Bishop said, separating us thinking there would be some fight between us. Ha, yeah right.

"What? I'm just wanting to get to know the newest guard. Give him a nice, Terminus Penitentiary welcome. Don't you think Bishop?" Calder said with a sarcastic grin.

"I've been here for a little over a month now, Havard. I'm not that new anymore," I said in mild irritation. I knew he was doing and saying this shit on purpose, trying to get a rise out of me, and I hated to admit that it was working.

"You're new enough. Besides, I bet you'd enjoy my personal welcome," Calder said with a smirk.

Yeah, based on the look in his eyes, his 'welcome' had to do with him and I locked up in his cell together, me pinned on his bed beneath him, and the both of us naked. Stupid sexy pervert.

"And I bet that you'd like to know that, wouldn't you?" I pressed on, wanting to see just how far I could push him before he snapped. Which wasn't far based on the growl he let out before he went to charge me, but Bishop stepped back in front of me again.

"Okay you two, that's enough!" Bishop snapped, fed up with us and our 'fighting'.

"Alright, Bishop, sorry. But it's pretty fun to get him all riled up," I said to Bishop as he looked at me like I was one screw shy of losing my mind. But when I glanced back up at Calder, he was biting his bottom lip as he stared at me before quickly mouthing to me.

"You're fucked. I want my damn kiss."

I couldn't stop the snort that came out of my mouth at that, finding his little threat amusing.

"You okay, Darby?" Bishop asked, looking at me in mild concern. I'm sure he thought I was definitely crazy now.

"Yeah, I'm good. I'm going to go get something to drink, I'll be back," I said, slipping my emotionless mask back into place.

"Alright."

As I walked off, I let my mask slip just enough to smirk at Calder who was still staring at me.

I may have just lost my supposed best friend, but honestly, screwing around with Calder is pretty damn fun.

I don't regret a single thing.

Possessive

S crewing with Calder yesterday was fun, especially with Bishop standing right there next to us, thinking that Calder might swing at me.

For the rest of the night last night, Calder kept trying to get me to go somewhere private with him so that he could 'get the kiss I owed him'. But I purposely avoided him just to further annoy him which was a success since after I had left this morning for shift change, he had texted me on the cell phone that he had hidden somewhere. He swore that today he was getting the kiss he was owed and then some, which made me laugh.

Just to further frustrate and aggravate him, I didn't reply to his text. I had only read it before getting out of the message thread, and then off my phone entirely so that I could sleep before later getting up for the rest of the day before I needed to head back to the Penitentiary for work.

When I woke up hours later, he had texted me a handful of times more, saying that I had better answer him 'or else'. Pfft, like I was scared of him. He wouldn't do a damn thing to me that I couldn't handle my own on.

After taking a shower, I went on my phone to look at some appliance websites before finally ordering myself a TV and oven, even splurging on same-day delivery since I had finally earned enough money to afford them.

I got dressed as I waited for my deliveries, and just an hour and a half later, the delivery men arrived and set up both my oven and TV, taking my other two away before leaving. It had taken them so long to finish that by the time they finally had left, it was time for me to head out to the Penitentiary.

I grabbed my things and then hurried out the door and to my car before speeding off to the Penitentiary, being careful not to go too far over the speed limit. I enjoyed working in a Penitentiary, but I doubted I would like an extended stay in such a place.

When I finally got there and parked, I jogged all the way to the unit and into the guards' office. Once I had made it inside, I headed straight back to my locker to put away my things.

"Cutting it close there, Darby, eh?" Patrick teased.

"Yeah, I know. Sorry, I got a new TV and oven today and got it delivered, and the guys took forever to install them, which is why I was almost late," I explained.

"We're just messing with you, but we're glad that you got that sorted," Ryan said with a grin.

"Yeah, me too," I chuckled with a slight shake of my head. "I'm going to head out there now. See you guys," I said.

"See you," Patrick said.

"Have fun out there," Ryan said after.

I couldn't help but chuckle at Ryan's words as I headed back out to the main area. I did my slow walk around the perimeter, watching over all of the inmates. I was in the process of walking passed the same back hallway area as yesterday when a hand locked around my wrist and tugged hard, sending me flying back down the hallway before I was pinned between the wall and a large, firm body. It was a no-brainer to me of who it was.

"So you think you can get away with not giving me my kiss and then ignoring me, do you?" Calder asked, making me smirk as I looked up at him and the scowl he wore.

"What? I've been busy today," I shrugged nonchalantly.

"But you read them," he pressed, getting more worked up.

"I did," I agreed.

"And you couldn't type out a response? Even just a simple okay or sorry?" He asked, aggravated.

"Nope, and besides, I have nothing to be sorry for. I did nothing wrong."

He growled, pressing his body against mine more before slamming his lips to mine as he kissed the living shit out of me. The kiss was so hard that it had my legs shaking, threatening to give out from under me at the shockwaves of heat it was causing to surge throughout my body. I moved my hands up his large, muscular arms, stopping to squeeze his shoulders before I continued to move my hands up, tangling them in his soft, blonde hair. I couldn't help but chuckle against his lips as a thought popped into my head, making him pull back and look at me like I had lost my mind for laughing in the midst of our heated kiss.

"What's so funny?" He asked gruffly.

"Just what we're doing right here, right now," I sighed with a lazy grin.

"Which is making out in the back hallway in secret?" He asked out in confusion.

"Well yeah, but we're both guys, and you're blonde," I laughed softly as I rested my head back against the wall, looking up at him.

"Yeah, I'm well aware of that," he said, still not getting it. Though I didn't really expect him to.

"Yeah, but I've never liked blondes. They've always been so...yuck to me," I explained.

"Oh? And am I yuck too?" He said, sounding the tiniest bit offended, making me bite my lip to keep from laughing. I shook my head as I continued to run my fingers through his hair, making him tilt his head back, happy that I didn't find him yuck. Though if we're honest, why would I do all this stuff with him if I did? He's not the brightest at times, but that's because he is a blonde after all.

"No. You are not and that's why I'm laughing. You're the only blonde I've ever been with."

"And the ONLY blonde that you'll ever be with!" He growled possessively as he pinned me even further against the wall.

"Oh yeah? Says who?" I said, testing him.

"I DO! You don't get to be with anyone else but me!" He snarled.

"Really now? Because whatever this is? This is just some fun. We're not together, so if I decide I'm done, then I'm done and you can't do a damn thing about it."

"You think you're funny, don't you? There's no one else that makes you feel like I do. You even told me as much that I'm the only one who gets you hard anymore. So I'm not worried about you ending whatever this is," he said cockily before his lips were back on mine as he kissed me aggressively, biting and pulling at my lips as he pressed impossibly closer to me, his hips lightly grinding and pressing against me.

I let out a low, happy moan as I tilted my head more to kiss him deeper and allow his prodding tongue more entry and room to roam, earning myself a happy grunt from him.

"Alright, come on you two. Quit sucking face," Gunnar suddenly said, interrupting us. I looked over seeing that both he and Bo were coming from around the corner.

"Yeah, you got a call, Calder," Bo said, making Calder grunt as he gave me another hard, toe-curling kiss before pulling back.

"Fuck, fine. And Darby, you pull that shit again and I'm going to fuck your ass up," Calder warned me.

"Ha! That's what you think!" I laughed as I slipped out from under him, hurrying back out to the main area and acting like I was there the entire time.

I was walking a few feet away from the right side wall when I felt a hand grab hold of my ass. I jerked my head to the side quickly, seeing that it was just Calder walking beside me with Bo and Gunnar on his other side who rolled their eyes at him.

"Remember whose ass this is," he muttered before he continued on his way passed me, heading over to one of the phones.

His words had set my body on fire, and I fucking hated to admit it, but I wanted him to fuck me and I wanted him to fuck me badly.

Faðir

- -

Calder's POV -

I was trying to behave in front of the other guards and inmates so no one would catch on to the fact that I was on the verge of fucking Darby, But, damn, does he make it hard. He looks so damn good in that ugly guard uniform.

"So, what's this call about?" I asked after I finally managed to pull my thoughts away from Darby and his ass.

"Not sure," Gunnar said with a shrug.

That fucking helps.

"Well, who's calling for me?" I asked, hoping that they at least knew that much since they didn't know what the call was about.

"Your Faðir," Bo said simply.(Father)

Ah, fuck!

When my Faðir calls that normally means trouble of some sort, mainly me getting in trouble with him for something. And I think I have an idea of what this call is about.

"Why didn't you fucking lead with that?!" I growled out in frustration as I walked faster to the one unoccupied phone.

"Probably because you always flip your shit when he's brought up," Gunnar muttered as I picked up the phone, glaring at him as I did so.

"Where the fuck have you been?!" Was snarled down the line the moment I opened my mouth to speak once the line connected.

"Hello to you too, Faðir. I'm good, thanks for asking," I said sarcastically as I rolled my eyes.

"Fuck off with the attitude with me. When do you plan on getting out? I retired for a reason which was to not have to do this shit anymore, and then you went and fucking got arrested, dipshit!" My Faðir growled in annoyance.

"Yes, Faðir, I fucking know that! I will be out when I decide the time is right!" I replied lowly, but Bo and Gunnar, who were standing behind me, scoffed at each other in amusement.

"Yeah right! More like when he's done having fun with a certain guard!" Bo cackled as he bumped shoulders with Gunnar.

"You're so not wrong there!" Gunnar agreed, joining him in laughing and nudging him back.

I jerked around, glaring at them as they continued cackling with each other like they had said the funniest damn thing in the world.

"Shut the fuck up!" I shouted at them, having had enough of them and their games.

"Guard? What guard? What the fuck are they talking about?!" My Faðir questioned, having heard their comments.

Fan-fucking-tastic. Thanks, assholes.

"Nothing, Faðir! It's just Bo and Gunnar talking out of their asses as usual!" I said, hoping to deter him, but I had no such luck.

"Yeah, well they normally speak the truth so I want to know what the fuck they are going on about!"

I pulled the phone receiver away from my mouth as I gave them both murderous glares that made them shut up instantly.

"I'm going to beat the living hell out of the two of you after this!" I seethed, watching them gulp worriedly.

"We're going to go look for Officer Kelby and ask him for something," Bo said worriedly.

"Yeah, mainly for protection," Gunnar added before they ran off, leaving me to come out to my Faðir.

"CALDER! ANSWER ME DAMMIT!" He was screaming as I put the phone back up to my ear, making me scowl.

"I'm right here, stop yelling in my damn ear!" I grumbled.

"Then start explaining what the two fífls were saying about you and a guard!" He shot back heatedly.(fools)

I sighed and pinched the bridge of my nose in frustration before speaking in Icelandic to ensure that no one nearby heard what I was saying.

"Það er þessi nýi vörður hér í Hegningarhúsinu og við hittumst einhvern veginn einslega, þó að við séum ekki beint saman. Meira eins og að fokka," I said, waiting for him to start screaming at me and saying I was a disgrace or something, but he did quite the opposite.(There's this new guard here at the Penitentiary and we are kind of seeing each other secretly, even though we're not exactly dating. More like fucking around.)

"Er hann góður í rúminu?"(Is he any good in bed?)

I was appalled by his question. That was the last thing I had ever expected him to say.

"Uh, um,jæja, við höfum ekki fokið ennþá, aðallega bara kysst."(Uh, um, well, we haven't fucked yet, mainly just kissed.)

"Jæja, hættu að spila leiki og fokka honum, sonur!"(Well, stop playing games and fuck him, son!)

"Ég er ringlaður. Ertu ekki reiður yfir því að ég sé að bulla með strák?"(I'm confused. You're not pissed that I'm screwing around with a guy?)

"Nei. Af hverju ætti ég að vera það? Mér er sama hver þú ert með eða hverjum þú ríða. Það er þitt val, ekki mitt."(No. Why would I be? I don't give a fuck who you're with or who you fuck. That's your choice to make, not mine.)

"Jæja, allt í lagi þá. Ég fer bráðum út, Faðir, svo ekki hafa áhyggjur."(Well, okay then. I'll be out soon, Father, so don't worry.)

"Allt í lagi þá. Bless."(Okay then. Bye.)

"Bless."(Bye.)

I hung up the phone, standing there for a second, baffled by the fact that my dad didn't seem to give a flying fuck that I was sort of with a guy and sort of gay.

I walked off, looking for Bo and Gunnar to tell them that they better consider themselves lucky that my Faðir didn't care that I was spending my days, really nights, with a guy, or even that he was a guard here at the Penitentiary.

I turned and saw them both standing slightly behind Darby who was looking annoyed at their presence, and I couldn't blame him. I walked over to them, seeing Bo and Gunnar stepping further behind him and noticing the rising tent in his uniform pants as he saw me approaching.

"Are you here to finally take these two fools away from me?" Darby asked, raising a brow and ignoring the fact that he not only had an erection but that I could see it.

"Hey! I thought we were bonding!" Bo cried out like a pouting child.

"Why would we be bonding? Didn't you come over here to get away from him since you, and I quote, 'said something that pissed him off that could end up with the both of us dead'?" Darby said, giving them a droll stare that had me raising an eyebrow.

"Oh, really?" I said.

"Yeah! And when you get pissed off, you're pretty damn scary!" Gunnar inputted.

"Good!" I said, but then Darby scoffed, letting out a slight chuckle that captured my attention.

"He's not scary in the least bit," he said, making Bo and Gunnar look at him like he had been smoking something and was high as hell.

"What the fuck are you talking about?! He's scary as hell!" Bo very nearly shrieked.

"No. He's really not," Darby shrugged which prompted me to take a few steps closer to him, reaching my hand out to discretely brush the backside of my hand along his erection, watching as his eyelids fluttered slightly as he just barely bit into his bottom lip from the pleasure.

"I've changed my mind," I said suddenly after looking at his erotic face.

"In regards to what?" He grunted out as I continued to rub my hand up against him.

"I'm not letting you have any more time to decide when you're ready, we're fucking tomorrow," I said simply which had his eyes snapped open wide. I could see the mix of shock, fear, and most of all, lust, shining brightly in his eyes.

"Hold the fuck up. Why?" He asked.

"You're too damn sexy. I need to fuck you and I can't wait any longer," I grunted at him, feeling my own erection throbbing painfully between my legs.

"Okay," he said as he gulped, making me smirk as I patted his erection, similar to the way would a pet.

"I'll let you get back to work now. But be prepared for tomorrow because the moment you walk through those doors, you are going to walk straight up to my cell. I'll be waiting for you," I husked out to him lowly watching as he, again, gulped and nodded at me.

"Okay. Until tomorrow," he said breathlessly.

"Yes. Until then," I said as I turned and walked back to my normal table with Bo and Gunnar trailing after me, looking at me in shock.

"I was not expecting to be standing there when you two decided on when to fuck," Gunnar said with a shake of his head.

"What do you mean when they decided to fuck? That was Calder deciding and Darby just going along with it!" Bo exclaimed to which I shrugged my shoulders as I, not so subtly, stared at Darby.

"He may act all tough now, but come tomorrow night, there's not a doubt in my mind that he'll submit to me in every way," I said with a smirk, and from behind me I heard Bo, as childish as ever say:

"Yeah, I'm sure there will be lots of cumming from the two of you tomorrow."

Preparing

Darby's POV -

Okay, I'm officially shit scared and horny as fuck at the exact same time.

I can't believe that he just walked over to me and said that we were going to be having sex tomorrow. And I agreed immediately! I didn't even take into consideration that I don't know a damn thing about how gay sex works! Something very vital when it comes to having gay sex!

What do I need to bring? Do I need to prepare myself in any way? Shit, I'm going to be losing my fucking anal virginity! Am I going to be able to walk normally afterward, much less stand up?

I had so many worries rushing through my head that it made the rest of the night fly by. That wasn't something that normally happens since the inmates get locked up in their cells for bed at about 10, sometimes a little later or earlier depending on if any fights occur, and then after that the Penitentiary is dead silent and boring as fuck.

After my shift ended the next morning, I gathered all my shit together and hurried out to my car. After hopping inside, I quickly pulled out my phone to start doing some research on gay sex. And can I just say, that after sitting in my car for nearly half an hour, reading and watching videos on it, I'm not scared anymore. Instead, I'm on the brink of exploding in my fucking uniform pants from imagining Calder and me doing all of those things tonight.

The one thing that I'm not looking forward to, though, is going and buying lube and condoms. That's going to be awkward, but there is no way in hell I was going to let him cum in my ass, at least not the first time Great, now I'm already thinking about fucking with him again and we haven't even done it the first time!

"Aw, fuck! I don't know what size condoms to buy him!" I groaned as I rested my forehead against the steering wheel for a moment before pulling out my phone, going to my message threads, and selecting the number that was connected to the phone he had. That reminded me that I still needed to figure out where the fucker had it hidden. But anyway, I fired off a quick text to him.

"I'm going to go buy shit for tonight so what size condoms do I need to buy for you?"

Never in my life would I have thought that I'd ever be asking another guy his dick size so I could buy him condoms, especially ones that he'll be wearing to fuck me. But hey, there's a first time for everything, and I'm finding that Calder is the first of lots of different things for me.

Not wanting to sit in the parking lot any longer and wait for that embarrassing response, I started my car and drove out of the parking lot, heading to the nearest store. After parking in a spot that was close to the store entrance, I sat petrified in my car. I was shit scared to see the way other people would look at me once they saw me grab the things I needed, but I was trying to focus on other things at the moment to not cause an anxiety attack. With a final sigh, I got out of my car, making sure to pocket my phone before I got out, and walked inside. I instantly headed to what I like to call the 'sex supply section'.

I was hoping that given how early it was, I could get what I needed and leave without being seen. But the moment I got to the aisle, I almost turned around and walked away when I saw a guy and a girl, obviously a couple, down there in the exact same spot that I needed to be.

At that exact time, my phone buzzed in my back pocket, and, assuming it was a text back from Calder, I pulled it out. But when I did, I saw that it was in fact Calder, but that he was calling instead. Fan-fucking-tastic.

"Great, this is going to be wonderful," I muttered as I accepted the call and brought the phone up to my ear. "Hello?" I said, and as soon as he spoke, I could immediately hear the smirk in his voice.

"You can't wait to see my dick, so now you want to know how big I am?"

I groaned at his words, but I wasn't entirely surprised that he had said that. I had begun to predict the type of crap that flew, unfiltered, out of his mouth.

"I'm not going over this on the phone with you while I'm in the store. What do I need to buy you?" I asked.

"Wait, what are you buying again?" He asked, and God did I want to throttle him so hard that his face turned blue.

"Calder, don't make me say it again," I seethed lowly.

"Either you say it and tell me what it is that you want to know, or you don't and you leave without whatever you want and you don't have it later. Your choice," he said. Goddamn him! He's doing this shit on purpose so that he can force me to say it knowing that I'm not ready for him to go into my ass without a condom, raw. "And don't think about trying to whisper it because I won't hear you."

He was enjoying this way too damn much, the bastard.

I groaned as I steeled myself before quickly speaking the words I needed to say, making sure he understood everything that I was saying so I wouldn't have to repeat it again.

"I'm at the store trying to buy things for tonight and I need to know what size condoms to buy you," I said, my voice monotone. I wasn't going to give him any further satisfaction.

"See? That wasn't so hard, now was it?" He asked, a grin easily decipherable in his voice.

I looked and saw a few nearby people looking at me, making me wish the floor would open and swallow me whole.

"Easy for you to say. Now can you tell me the size so I can buy them and go home and sleep?!" I snapped, my patience evaporating into thin air.

"Alright, alright. There's no way you're falling asleep later, so fine. Get the XXXL ones."

My eyes nearly shot clean out of my head as I stopped in the middle of the aisle at his words.

"Come again? I think I misheard you," I said to which he chuckled.

"XXXL. What? You scared?" He teased.

"You're going to rip my ass apart!" I hissed into the phone as I hurriedly grabbed two boxes of condoms - one for him in his size, and the other for me in my size since I was not planning on cumming all over his cell and I had run out of ones in my size at home. I also grabbed five tubes of lube, wanting to have enough since I now know how big he is, and then I hurried out of the aisle, going to pay for my seven items.

"You'll enjoy it," he hummed cockily.

"Look, I have to go. See you tonight, bye."

"I will definitely be seeing you tonight," he chuckled as I promptly hung up on him.

I looked at the registers, trying to decide which one to go to, but then I saw the self-checkout and I hurried over to it. I quickly scanned the items and bagged them so no one could even catch a glimpse. Once I paid, I hurried out of the store and into my car, driving home quickly and climbing into bed.

I laid still for a while, forcing myself to calm down and relax so I could sleep before heading back into the Penitentiary again tonight, and most likely to the death of my asshole.

F*cking Things Up

I took a few deep breaths as I opened both boxes of condoms and slid a few of each size into the pockets of my uniform pants as I finished getting ready for work after my much-needed, long sleep. Then, I grabbed three tubes of lube and slid them into the chest pocket of my uniform shirt. I was more nervous about losing my anal virginity now than I was when I lost my, I don't know what to call it, I guess it's my dick virginity. I wasn't scared of being fucked by him before, but after he told me what size condoms to buy him, I started to freak the fuck out.

I grabbed the normal things that I always grabbed from home before leaving, and then walked out of my apartment, heading to my car. I climbed in and made my way to the Penitentiary, the drive seeming longer than normal today, and for that I was thankful. I just needed a little bit of extra time to prepare myself for later.

When I finally arrived and parked, I took in a long, deep breath before getting out, grabbing my things, and heading inside the office. I went straight through, barely stopping at each badge identification scanner before heading into my unit and then my locker in the guards' office. I placed my water bottle, keys, granola bar, phone, and wallet inside before shutting it and turning around to see Patrick, Ryan, and Bishop walking into the office.

"Hey Darby," Ryan greeted me just like he did every other day.

"Hey," I nodded back.

"How are you doing?" Patrick asked, to which I shrugged.

"Can't complain, how about you guys?" I replied though it was a complete lie. I was nervous and fucking horny, but I couldn't exactly say that without them asking questions I didn't want to give answers to.

"Doing good," Ryan grinned.

"Just fine," Patrick said.

"I'm doing fine," Bishop shrugged.

"That's good. I'm going to head out there and start working," I said as I went to head out when Bishop stopped me.

"Hey, wait a quick second. I wanted to ask you something right quick."

"Sure, what about?" I asked in slight confusion.

"Calder Havard."

It took everything in me to not tense or sallow or do anything to give away that I wasn't currently internally panicking at the mere mention of his name. Did Bishop know something?

"Okay. What about him?" I asked, acting as nonchalantly as possible without it coming off as fake.

"I noticed you, him, and his two friends, Bo and Gunnar, talking yesterday like you were old friends. I thought you two despised one another?" Bishop asked sounding both confused and curious. But I made sure to spin the truth into what I hoped would be a very likely and believable lie.

"More like a misunderstanding. If it could even be called that. He was giving me grief because I'm the newest guard and I took him down on my first day, but we're good now."

"Oh, okay. I mean, yeah, that would have probably pissed him off," Bishop chuckled, easily accepting my words.

"Yeah, it did," I agreed.

"But still, I have never seen him that, I guess, relaxed around a guard in my life. Nothing against you or anything, Darby, but we're just all surprised," Patrick said.

"Yeah, because in case you haven't noticed, he can be quite a dickhead," Ryan laughed to which I snorted softly.

"Yeah I noticed, and I don't know why he's so much more relaxed around me. Probably because he knows I won't tolerate his bullshit," I said to which they all shrugged and nodded, not looking suspicious at all. "Okay, well, I'm headed out there. See you guys later," I said before I opened the door.

I exited the office quickly, shutting the door behind me before making my way along the edges of the main area slowly as I headed towards the stairs. Once I reached them, I ascended them slowly to not draw any attention to myself, yet when I reached the top, Bo and Gunnar stood there looking like they were waiting for me.

"You better hurry and get to him. He's like a hungry lion with how much he keeps pacing in his cell," Gunnar said as they both chuckled while I rolled my eyes.

"He can wait. He seems to forget that I'm supposed to be working instead of being his secret fuck buddy."

"Yeah, you tell him that. It still wouldn't make him change," Bo said with a snort.

"Yeah, I know. Keep an eye out for me in case they come looking for me again?" I asked them.

"Don't worry, we've got you," Gunnar assured me.

"Yeah, but you better protect us if we do have to interrupt you two. Calder might kill us," Bo said.

"Alright, fine. I'll protect you if need be because you're probably right. I better get going," I said, watching the wide grins spread across their faces as I began to walk passed them.

"Have fun!" Gunnar winked.

"Don't scream too loud!" Bo added.

Again, I rolled my eyes as I walked down the hallway to Calder's cell. I opened his cell door, slipping inside quickly and quietly to see him pacing, just as they had said. But he stopped the moment I closed the door, despite having been dead silent when I had done so, and his eyes locked on me.

"About damn time!" He growled as he didn't hesitate to rush me and pin me to his cell door, beginning to kiss along my exposed neck and throat.

"Calm yourself or I'll turn and leave right now," I threatened, but I had to fight down the moan that threatened to slip out at his rough treatment of me.

"You try that and I won't hesitate to rip your uniform off of you and pound you senseless before you could even hallway turn," he threatened, making me shudder at his whispered words against my throat, his hands moving to unbutton my uniform shirt.

"Hold on...here," I said as I reached into the chest pocket of my shirt, producing the three tubes of lube I brought, making him smirk down at me hungrily.

"Anything else you want to give me so that I can finish stripping you down?"

I put either of my hands in each of my pockets, pulling out the four condoms of each size that I had shoved in them earlier.

"There, that's it," I said through a slight pant.

He looked at the multiple condoms and tubes of lube before eying me up with a seductive smirk that had my cock leaking like a faucet and pulsing with my desire for him.

"Did you intend on us going multiple rounds?" He asked, my eyes widening as my cheeks went a little red.

"N-No! I was just trying to be prepared!" I practically squeaked out. At this point, I didn't even know what I was thinking. I was too far gone, having been too consumed by my desire for him.

"Sure, sure. But just in case you were wondering, I'm more than willing to go multiple rounds with you," he winked.

"We haven't even fucked for the first time yet and you're already going on about additional rounds!" I cried out in disbelief before gulping nervously. The sad part was how fucking tempted it already sounded to me, not even knowing what exactly I was about to get myself into. For all I know he could paralyze me!

"What do you say we go ahead and change that then?" He asked, quickly placing the condoms and tubes of lube on the nearby cement desk. Once he did that, he turned back to face me and proceeded to strip my uniform off, not stopping until I was left standing in just my boxers before I moved to help him do the same. With him nearly naked, I couldn't help myself but stop and admire him for a moment.

His chest and arms were tattooed with drawings that bled together seamlessly, all looking like they belonged there. There were just too many on him to discern what each was from the brief, hurried look I was giving him. But I did notice that the vast majority were just black and white with only small pops of color mixed in, and I was quite attracted to the tattoo the went across the front of his chest and up to his collarbones where there was the words Þetta Reddast, Icelandic words of some sort, with a raven tattooed at the beginning and end of the saying.

God, he looked amazing! Even with his boxers still on, I could see the outline of his large and thick cock. I knew that taking him would be difficult, but I was bound and determined to do so. I had tried to fight it for too long, and now that I had the chance, I wasn't going to let it slip through my fingers.

"Hurry up, Calder!" I said as I practically dove into his arms, slamming our lips together. I eagerly pressed myself against him making him growl as he turned and pressed me down into the bed, pulling down both of our boxers while never once letting our lips separate. Instead, we pressed our lips together harder, practically sucking the air from one another's lungs.

He finally separated our lips when the need for air and each other became too much to bear as he hurriedly climbed off of the small bed to retrieve a tube of lube and a condom for each of us. With supplies in hand, he dove back on top of me, making me laugh at how ridiculous he was behaving.

It was almost like watching a child dive into a ball pit with how excited he looked.

"Well, aren't you eager?" I smiled up at him.

"Yes! Especially since I don't know how long it will take for me to prep you to take me!" He rushed out as he moved to begin removing the seal of the lube. As I looked back down, I was reminded of just how monstrous of a cock he had, and drooled some before gulping as the nervousness settled back in my gut.

"Yeah, well it's not my fault that you have a horse's cock attached to your body!" I snapped back at him, still not sure how or why a person could have a cock so large.

"You'll love it. Now, spread your legs for me," he demanded.

I spread my legs at his command and he pecked my lips in reward for complying before sliding slowly down my body, pressing kisses along as he went until he was nestled between my legs. His broad shoulders forced me to spread my legs even wider for him to be able to fit between them, his face just a few inches away from my leaking tip. All I wanted was for him to suck on the head of my cock and lick at my slit, just a little. Instead, he moved his hands down to my ass cheeks and spread them wide open, giving him a full view of my tight hole that clenched in anticipation of what was to come.

He looked up from staring at my hole to lock eyes with mine as he licked his lips before dropping his head down suddenly. He buried his face between my cheeks as his tongue greedily lapped at my hole, rimming it, before he pushed his tongue inside me making me cry out from the intense pleasure. The feeling of his warm, wet tongue pressing against my insides was so good, almost too good to the point that I worried I might lose consciousness and miss out on this amazing feeling.

At my cries of pleasure, he reached up behind my head and jerked the flat pillow out from under my head, pressing it to my face in an attempt to muffle my moans and cries of pleasure, but not to suffocate me. As he did that, he didn't stop pleasuring my hole making me leak more now than I ever have before. The feeling was just incredible.

"C-Calder...mmm, fuck! I-I'm going to cum- mmm!" I moaned, excited to finally feel my pent-up release explode out of me. But it never did because he was suddenly pulling his tongue out of me, smirking as he licked his lips yet again making them shimmer and shine enticingly at me.

"I have to say, your ass tastes so much better than any pussy I've ever had. Which is why I can't have you cumming yet, because it will just ruin the fun," he said.

I struggled to keep my irritation down at the mention of him eating pussy when he was just tongue-deep in my ass. For some reason, it made my chest feel tight and ache in the slightest bit, but I pushed the feelings aside to focus on what was currently going on.

"Calder, I'm begging you, please hurry up and prep me so you can fuck me!" I begged.

"Someone's a little desperate," he smirked which made me glare at him aggravatedly. No shit, I was so desperate, and I'm not afraid to admit it anymore either. I wanted him, and I wanted him so damn bad!

"Calder please!"

Having heard enough of my begs and pleas, he grabbed the tube of lube he had already unsealed earlier and popped open the lid. He squirted a large amount on my hole and then applied even more on three of his fingers which I knew would be going inside of me shortly.

Without a word, he pushed a single finger inside of me, making me groan and bite down on his pillow as he began to slowly move it in and out of me. It felt strange and uncomfortable at first but then it started to feel good as I lightly rocked back onto his hand. Just when I had finally started to get used to his first finger, he pushed in a second finger, poking and prodding my insides with them in tandem, making me writhe and my back arch off the mattress as I struggled to keep quiet.

He only had two fingers in me, stretching me out, and still had one to go. If I was struggling to remain quiet now, what the fuck was I going to do when he finally put his dick in me?!

While I was absorbed in my thoughts, he began to push his third finger into me. The moment he had fully pushed it in, I felt him press against something inside of me that nearly had me screaming screaming. This pleasure was something that I'd never felt before. It was even better than getting rimmed, which I hadn't thought was possible!

"Ahhhh-ohhmmmmm!" I moaned into the pillow as I pushed my ass further into his poking and prodding fingers, trying to get more of that addictive pleasure that only he could give me.

"Fuck, you're so sexy!" He growled as he moved his fingers more urgently in and out of me, just like I wanted.

"C-Calderrr..." I moaned as I felt my release nearing, but yet again, he pulled away from me leaving me even more needy than before.

"Fuck, finally I can get into your ass!" He growled as he grabbed his condom and ripped it open, sliding it down onto his shaft. I grabbed a condom for my cock, opened it, and put it on so that I wouldn't make an even bigger mess than I had already.

He rose to his knees and grabbed the backs of my thighs, slightly lifting my ass off of the bed. He rubbed his covered cock against my hole which had me shivering as my hole clenched in anticipation. I took a few breaths to calm myself down, knowing that tightening up would only make things worse for myself, and looked up at Calder who was already staring down at me, giving him a nod.

"Go."

At my one-word affirmation, he began to slowly push his cock inside me. Fuck it hurt like hell! It quite literally felt like someone was ripping my ass in two, and someone was: Calder Havard!

"Oh fucking hell! Fuck this feels fucking fantastic!" He groaned and moaned while I bit the hell out of his pillow to keep from screaming out in pain, a few tears falling from the corners of my eyes from the effort of holding back the pain. But it was just too much as I ripped the pillow from my face.

"C-Calder! S-Stop! Fuck, stop!" I grunted out in pain, unable to take it anymore. I needed a break, or a fucking icepack to soothe the fire I was feeling. Hell, a stretcher would be nice, too!

He immediately stopped pushing inside of me at my shout and took in my scrunched-up, pained face with worry.

"Shit! Darby, I'm sorry I wasn't paying attention! I should've stopped before, I was too focused on how good your ass felt around my cock! Are you okay?" He fretted, surprising me by how concerned he looked and sounded.

"It's okay. Just sit here for a minute please, so that I can get used to your size," I panted.

"Of course, Darby, anything for you," he said as he reached down and wiped away the few tears that had fallen from my eyes before dropping his head to give my lips a gentle peck. He rested his forehead on mine as his hands slowly moved up and down my sides, relaxing me as I felt my ass adjusting to accommodate his massive cock.

"Mmm...m-move Calder. Please move. I'm ready for you," I pleaded once I felt ready.

"You sure?" He asked, and in response, I wrapped my arms around his neck and my legs around his waist, lifting my hips further to press against his.

"I'm positive...now fuck me, Calder."

He growled at me hungrily and began to slowly move inside of me. Before long, he began to pick up his pace, slamming into me so hard that my entire body began to burn and pulse with the pleasure of each of his powerful thrusts.

"Oooh, yes! Fuck, Darby, you're so tight! It feels so good!" He moaned as he dropped his head, biting and sucking at the skin on the base of my throat. He moved his mouth lower, latching onto one of my nipples, sucking at it roughly as his thrusts never wavered.

This man is a fucking machine, I tell you! He knows exactly what to do with that beast of his, and how to move his hips best so that I'm in complete bliss and not in any pain whatsoever. I mean, I could still be in pain, but the pleasure was overpowering any and every other feeling.

"Mmm! Calder, I'm going to cum!" I cried out.

"Fuck, me too! Cum with me now, elskan!"

I don't know what the fuck he said at the end, but he said to cum and I did, doing so completely untouched. I filled the condom I wore to catch my release, pumping out more cum than I'd ever seen come out of me. The condom was so full that it looked like it might spill out the bottom of it. Calder grunted as he laid down on top of my body since the tiny mattress didn't exactly have enough room for two grown men, much less one that was above the average build. We both panted, feeling spent after the best sex that either of us has ever had in our lives, at least it was on my end. Hopefully, it was on his end too, otherwise, that would be pretty fucking humiliating for me.

"Fuck, that was great!" I let out breathlessly.

"No kidding, elskan!" He chuckled against the crook of my neck, pressing a few kisses to my sweaty skin. I frowned upon hearing that same word from before.

"What do you keep saying?" I asked, curious to know the English translation of what was obviously a word from another language.

"What? Do you mean elskan?"

"Yeah, whatever that is."

"Elskan is Icelandic for either darling or baby," he translated.

"Oh? And you keep calling me that, why?" I asked.

"Because I can, elskan. What have I told you before? You're mine," he husked out possesively making me fight back shivers at just how serious he sounded. But I needed to know one thing before anything else could be said or done.

"I thought we were just fucking around and having fun, though?"

"Me too, but you felt how amazing that sex was. I can't just let you leave. Face it, you're now mine for however long I'd like."

My entire body stiffened at what he had said.

I know what I've been saying, and even just said. We were just doing this for some fun, but I think- no, scratch that, I KNOW that I like Calder.

Hearing that he wants me, but only just for how long he decides he wants to keep me around is making me panic. Regret over what we just did washed over me, nearly growing me like a tidal wave. I need to get out of here, and away from him. I can't be near him any longer, especially knowing that I'm just a temporary fix to him.

I quickly wiggled out from under him, pulling the condom off of my cock, and tossing it in the trash can he had in his cell. That in itself was weird since he's never had a trash can in here before, and as far as I know, inmates aren't allowed them in their cells for safety reasons. But I didn't let it deter me as I began to throw my uniform back on as quickly as I could.

"What the fuck, Darby? Where are you going?!" Calder semi-shouted in disbelief, sitting up in bed to watch me rushing about.

"Back to work, where I should have stayed. This shouldn't have happened. It was a mistake," I said, ignoring the pang I felt in my chest as I did so, at saying the complete opposite of how I actually felt. But I had to protect myself. I wouldn't let him break me or show any sign of weakness in front of him, no matter how difficult that was at the moment.

"Seriously, Darby?!" He continued to shout at me.

"Don't text, call, or even talk to me ever again. We should just go back to hating and ignoring each other like we should've done the entire time," I said as I finished getting dressed before opening his cell door and leaving quickly.

I looked forward with a cold look on my face, feeling stupid for ever having involved myself with him in the first place. I should have stuck to my guns. I shouldn't have been so weak.

"Hey, about time! How was it?" Gunnar grinned as I approached them where they still stood near the top of the stairs. But I couldn't say anything, if I did, I worried that I might crack and then I'd be screwed, and not in the way that had just taken place before. God, just thinking about it hurt so damn bad.

"Was it good?" Bo teased, but I ignored them both as I walked passed, hurriedly heading back downstairs.

"Darby?" Gunnar called out to me in confusion.

"You good?" Bo asked next.

No. I wasn't 'good' in the slightest.

Again, I ignored them.

I can't believe I was so stupid. And to think, I lost my best and only friend because of him.

I'm such a dumbass! What have I done?!

Lost in Translation

Calder's POV -

What the fuck just happened?!

We both agreed that we just had the best sex of our lives together, I told him that he was mine (like I normally do), and then he got stiff as fuck, zoned out, got up, and got dressed, leaving right after that as fast as he could. He looked like he had just gotten punched or something, not like he just got his entire world rocked like he should have!

I just don't fucking understand it!

I climbed off of my bed and pulled off my used condom, tossing it in the trash can he had tossed his in. I had put it in my room earlier so that we had a place to discard the condoms that I knew we would use, and I seriously doubted that we'd have been able to sneak them downstairs. After what just happened though, I was just completely lost and needed to know what was going on, which is why I was getting dressed as fast as I could. I planned on chasing him down and getting him to talk to me about what the hell just happened.

Now fully redressed, I opened my cell door and rushed out and down the hall to the stairs where both Bo and Gunnar stood. They were looking at each other in confusion, speaking lowly to themselves.

"Where is he?!" I asked, the aggravation clear as day on my face.

"He went back downstairs to the main area. We tried to talk to him but he just walked right passed us without a word," Gunnar said in mystification.

"Yeah, and he looked pissed off as all hell. What the fuck happened in there?" Bo asked me, looking lost. I threw my hands up in the air, the answer a mystery to even me, at least for now.

"Fuck if I know! That's why I need to find him and talk to him!"

"I don't think he wants to talk to you," Gunnar said. As if I was going to listen to that kind of bullshit. Not a chance in hell.

"Well, too fucking bad because I want to talk to him!" I said as I started to descend the stairs with them trailing behind me. My eyes scanned the main area in search of him, and when I finally spotted him, I felt my blood boil with rage. He was leaning against the wall near that dumb fuck, Enzo Lazzaro's, table. It didn't take a genius to know that he had chosen that spot on purpose, thinking that I wasn't going to go over there. But he underestimated me, my rage, and my determination to get an answer out of him.

"Kelby!" I growled as I stalked closer to him.

He looked at me with a cold look on his face that I'd never seen before, and then he turned to look away from me. I felt like I'd been hit by the way that he didn't look at me like normally did. It fucking hurt.

"Go away, Havard," he said with anger in his words that were directed at me, even though he wasn't even looking in my direction.

"No! We need to talk!" I growled at him insistently.

"About what? There's nothing to talk about. I'm just a guard here and you're an inmate. What do two total opposites even have to talk about?" He asked dully, though I could hear that his anger was still present.

I stepped closer to him, dropping my voice as I ignored the fact that there were others most likely witnessing what was going on. But I didn't give a single fuck. I wanted to know what happened. I needed to know, no matter what it took.

"Really? Because we just had the most mind-blowing sex, and then you got pissed over something and left me. What the fuck happened back there?!" I snarled.

"I don't know what you're talking about," he said, but I saw something in his eyes that resembled pain. He clenched his jaw, eyes still looking out at the main area and not where they should be directed: at me!

"That's a fucking lie and you kno-" I started again, only to be cut off.

"Well, well, well. What's going on over here, Havard? Having a disagreement with Officer Kelby, are you?" The stupid fuck himself said from behind me, making me snarl at the mere sound of his annoying voice.

"Stay the fuck out of shit that doesn't concern you, Lazzaro!" I shouted as I whirled around to face him with a sneer contorting my features.

"But it does concern me, seeing as how you're talking to my favorite Penitentiary guard."

The fact that he said that MY Darby was HIS favorite guard set me off into an indescribable level of rage. I wasn't seeing red, I was seeing almost completely black I was so pissed at him, because how fucking dare he! I launched at him, taking him down to the ground easily as I repeatedly drove my fist into his face. With my other hand, I wrapped it around his throat, squeezing so tightly that I could see the blood vessels in his eyes beginning to bulge, threatening to burst bringing me a sick sort of happiness. He reached up, desperately trying to punch me but he was losing oxygen too fast to be able to do anything other than gasp for air like a dying fish. Good.

"CALDER THAT'S FUCKING ENOUGH!" Darby screamed at me as he dragged me off of Enzo, his strength always surprising me. But I couldn't dwell on that.

"NO! IT'S NOT FUCKING ENOUGH! I'M GOING TO FUCKING KILL THAT BASTARD!" I screamed back. I was on the warpath and I wanted blood. And only Lazzaro's would do. I wanted to see his blood spilled across the old cement floors and to see the life draining from his eyes.

"Enough with your shit! Bo, Gunnar, do something with your stupid ass boss!" Darby growled as he continued to drag me away from Lazzaro's writhing, gasping body while I struggled against Darby's hold. I wanted to go back after him again and finish the job for what he said about my Darby.

"You know that we can't stop him when he's like this. It's only..." Bo trailed off as he looked in between the two of us.

"Darby! Go put his ass in isolation!" Bishop suddenly shouted as he approached us with rushed steps.

"Yes, Bishop!" Darby spoke back as he started to drag me in the direction of isolation, but I never stopped fighting him every step of the way.

"Let me go, Darby! Let me kill him!" I growled.

"No! He didn't do a damn thing wrong!" He growled back. Wrong move, elskan.

"He said you were HIS favorite guard, and that's not fucking happening! YOU'RE MINE, DARBY, NOT HIS! " I bellowed at him as he pulled me down the empty hallway that led to isolation. I hoped the entire fucking Penitentiary heard me and knew to not touch him, speak to him, go near him, or even look at him.

"I'm no one's," he said through gritted teeth.

"Yes, you are, Darby! You're mine, elskan!" I insisted as I tried to jerk out of his grip to pin him to the wall, but he held me firm, having expected it.

"Enough with the elskan! It's not happening! There's no us so there's no need to call me by a pet name!" He sounded pissed, and as we neared isolation, I knew that I needed to try one more time to figure out what happened that made him flip so quickly. What I had said that set him off. I couldn't be sent away from him without fixing things, first.

"Darby, please, tell me what I did wrong! What did I say to upset you so much, so that I can fix it?!" I begged and pleaded with him desperately.

"You only said the truth, and I realized that it's better to not get further involved with you than I already have. I just wish I would have realized it before I let you fuck me," he said lowly just before handing me over to the guards in isolation.

I looked back at him, seeing that he wasn't even trying to hide or disguise the pain in his eyes. My chest constricted painfully, a feeling I had never felt before and wished to never have to feel ever again. I felt like I couldn't even breathe.

"Darby..." That was all I could say before I was pushed away from him and into a cell, leaving me alone with my thoughts as I wracked my brain on what I had said.

And then it hit me.

"Me too, but you felt how amazing that sex was. I can't just let you leave. Face it, you're now mine for however long I'd like."

It was the last line of what I had said that had caused all of the problems.

I had basically called him disposable, which wasn't true in the least bit. I was starting to realize that, now that it seemed he was gone, I needed him in my life. He kept me grounded. He kept me sane.

But I'm pretty sure that my stupidity has resulted in me losing what would have and should have been the best thing in my life. And it's all because I didn't phrase it better.

Getting Out

Calder's POV -

I have been stuck in isolation for almost a month now. I keep getting in fights with the guards who are supposed to check on me because I keep trying to leave this isolation bullshit to get back out to my elskan, Darby.

That's right, I called Darby my elskan, which means my darling baby because that's what he is: my darling baby.

I'm dying to get out of this shit-ass isolation so I can go drop down to my knees (something I never expected I'd ever do for someone in my life) and beg him to not leave me. To hear me out and know that I want to be with him. And not just for some temporary fun. I want us to try for something real. I didn't care that everyone would see, and I didn't care how weak I would look. Because without him, I was nothing.

After 6:00 PM tonight, I was finally getting released. What's better is that is when Darby will be here coming in for his shift. I was going to go straight to him and I was going to beg for another chance, for him to be and stay as mine. No matter what it took.

A guard finally came and got me, and I was practically running to get back out to the main area and to him. When I finally did reach the main area, my head was swiveling rapidly as I swung my head around, desperately searching for my elskan.

"Calder, we need to talk to you," Gunnar said as he and Bo hurried over to me as I continued my search for Darby. But I wasn't going to be swayed from my current task.

"Maybe later, right now I'm busy," I brushed them off impatiently.

"Calder, this can't wait! It's really important!" Bo said urgently. But I waved him off too as I continued to look for Darby.

"Look, I really don't have time to talk. I really need to find Darby and talk to him," I said as I went to hurry off to scour the main area for him. But before I could go more than two steps, both Bo and Gunnar grabbed each of my arms, holding me back and giving me twin looks of sympathy and pity which had me frowning in confusion.

"What? What the fuck is it?" I asked, irritated by their looks and interruption in my search.

"Calder, it's about Darby," Gunnar said a bit hesitantly.

I perked up at the mention of my elskan.

"Darby? What about Darby? Tell me now!" I demanded.

They sighed and then Bo spoke, saying what has to be the most devastating words that I have ever heard in my life.

"Calder...Darby doesn't work here anymore. He quit a few days after you got sent into isolation."

I felt like I had been punched in the gut repeatedly, maybe even kicked a few times too as all of the air in my lungs dissipated. I could practically feel my heart cracking in my chest at hearing that he wasn't here. But I just couldn't believe it, I didn't want to.

"W-What? He-He's GONE?! He can't be gone! He just CAN'T be!" I cried out, feeling myself on the verge of hyperventilating from the stress.

"I'm sorry Calder. But he is," Gunnar apologized sadly.

I shook my head before I turned and hurried up the stairs, going straight into my cell where everything had been so amazing the month prior before all going to shit in an instant, slamming the door behind me. I began to punch and kick the wall angrily, feeling nothing but pure rage take over me, washing the devastation away from me.

He'd left me. He was really gone. And the worst part of it all was that he had done it while I was locked up in isolation so he wouldn't have to see me. So that I wouldn't know as I sat in there, trying to come up with a way to get out there to see him, only for him to not even be there anymore!

My cell door swung open and in ran both Bo and Gunnar, looking at me worriedly.

"Calder, just relax. Maybe it's for the best that he lef-" Bo started, but I cut him off, not wanting to hear whatever bullshit was getting ready to come out of his mouth.

"Don't fucking finish that sentence! It's not for the best! I need him! HE'S MINE! I don't care what I have to do, but I'm getting the fuck out of here, and I'm going to find him! He's not getting away from me!" I growled wildly.

"Wait, we're finally going to bust the hell out of here?!" Gunnar hissed quietly so no one would hear him accidentally, but he sounded excited.

"Yes! I need to get to him and tell him that I'm an idiot and I fucked up, but I need to have him in my life!" I said determinedly.

"Does that mean you want you and Darby to have, like, a real relationship?" Bo asked with a slight twitch to his lips.

"Yes. I need to call my Faðir because the three of us are getting the fuck out of here as soon as the sun rises," I said as I exited my cell and headed straight down to the phones. I may or may not have shoved a few people out of the way, but who gives a fuck. I was on a mission.

Bo and Gunnar grinned wickedly as I grabbed a phone, and placed a call to my dad who picked up a few moments later.

"Calder?"

"Yeah, Faðir, it's me. Get the shit ready because Bo, Gunnar, and I want out tomorrow at sunrise," I said, my voice hard but quiet.

"About fucking time! We'll have everything set and ready to go," he said. I could practically hear the smirk in his voice as he spoke, thrilled that he could go back to enjoying his 'retirement'.

"Sounds good. See you soon on the outside," I said with a smirk.

"Yes, see you," he said, and then I hung up the phone as I turned and looked at Bo and Gunnar who were waiting anxiously to hear what the plan was, and whether or not we were getting out.

"We better rest up because tomorrow morning, after more than five years, we're finally going to be free of this place," I said.

"Fuck yes!" Gunnar cheered.

"I can't wait to get out!" Bo hooted.

And I can't wait to get Darby back.

Guess Who's Back

I thought I was alone when Grant left me before, but I'm even more alone now since I decided to quit working at the Penitentiary. As much as I had enjoyed working there, I did it so that I wouldn't have to be with or around...him anymore.

I couldn't even say or think his name without my chest hurting like hell because of how damn badly I missed him and all the things we had done. But I wasn't going back to him. I couldn't, not after finding out about his true intentions.

I needed to stay away from him even though I was in pain. I bet that after another month or so, I would be fine and I wouldn't even think about him and how damn handsome he is, or how he's so cocky that it's funny, or how damn good he fucked me.

Yeah, I'm totally lying to myself. I doubt that I'll ever get over him, but for my sake and my own sanity, it's best if I do just that. Things wouldn't have ended well since we both wanted very different things. He just wanted to have fun while I wanted something real. It just couldn't and wouldn't have worked out, what with him being in the Penitentiary and me being employed by it.

After I had quit working at the Penitentiary, having no choice, I went back to the bar I had been bartending for and started working there again. The managers were all too happy to have me back since, apparently, there were a few customers who weren't too happy that I had left. But because I needed a source of income and I knew they were almost always short-staffed, I went back. And I still hate it just as much as I did when I first worked there. The Penitentiary was the best place and I loved working there with Bishop, Patrick, and Ryan, but I screwed that all up and had to leave.

Today, thankfully, I was off from bartending and I was more than thrilled with that since my sleep schedule was all screwed up. It was mainly because I was having trouble sleeping but I wasn't sure why. I still worked at night which meant I slept during the day, just like when I used to work at the Penitentiary, so I don't know what the problem is.

I had just finished eating my breakfast, a simple ham and cheese omelet, and sat down on my couch after washing my plate. I turned on the TV, seeing BREAKING NEWS flashing across the screen the moment it came on. Seconds later, a news anchor was popping up on the screen with a serious yet grim expression on his face.

I wonder who died this time, I thought as I knew these reports typically happened when big-name people died.

"Good morning, Las Vegas! My name is Martin Douglass and I'm here in the studio with some Breaking News coming from Terminus Penitentiary!" The anchor announced, making me focus more on the TV at the mention of my previous workplace. "We have received word from our on-site reporters that there was a commotion out in front of the Penitentiary at 7:00 AM this morning that ended up with the escape of three inmates from the Penitentiary!"

I shot up to my feet as panic and dread washed over my body in tidal waves, already having a feeling of who the escaped inmates were. Soon after my worries were confirmed as they announced the names with pictures.

"We have just been given the names of the three inmates who have escaped the Penitentiary, as well as their correlating pictures. These inmates are Bo Torsten, Gunnar Halfdan, and finally, Calder Havard," the news anchor, Martin, said as their pictures appeared one right after the other once each of their names were said.

Oh fuck, it's about to be me dying.

"Fuck, fuck, and fuck! This can't be fucking happening right now!" I cried out as I began to run my fingers through my hair, pulling on the strands. I paced back and forth in worry as my stress levels rose to soaring new heights.

I turned and ran to my bedroom to go and take a shower to calm myself. I felt a little better knowing that he at least didn't know where I lived. Plus, I had changed my phone number the day I quit, so he couldn't text or call me. I had nothing to worry about.

I climbed in the shower and put the water almost to scalding and climbed in, wanting to wash and burn away all my stress. And I did, sighing as I felt much more relaxed than I did before my shower. I went over to my closet, putting on some clean, comfy clothes that consisted of a soft, long-sleeved grey shirt and a pair of cotton shorts. With my skin pink and still warm from my shower, and dressed in the comfiest set of clothes that I owned, my previous worries vanished as I relaxed. I was ready to go plant myself back on my couch, turn the TV on some stupid sitcom or another, and take a nap to make up for my recent lack of sleep.

Just as I was about to plant myself down on the couch, there was a soft knock on my apartment door that had me frowning in confusion. I hadn't the faintest idea who it could be since I didn't talk to anyone. My parents and I exchanged texts or talked on the phone, but I had kind of been ignoring my phone lately, and I didn't have any friends since Grant had been the only person I could stand, up until recent events that is. Normally, it was people who were trying to sell me shit I didn't need, or people looking for my neighbor's apartment but always wound up coming to mine instead. It happens a lot more often than you would think.

So, I redirected myself from going to sit on the couch to going over to my front door to see who was knocking on it. I took a deep breath, preparing myself to give the same speech about how 'this is the wrong apartment, you're looking for XYZ's ' before I finally decided to just get it over with, and opened the door.

I didn't even have a chance to really look at the person to see who it was or say anything when I opened up my front door since I was pushed back into my apartment as they came rushing in, leaving me standing there gaping at them in shock. It wasn't until they had shut and locked my apartment door behind them that I finally managed to shake off my surprise as I grew pissed at this mystery person's intrusion.

"Hey! What the fuck is going on?!"

And then I finally caught sight of the tall, muscular body that was covered in what was supposed to be baggy and oversized all-black clothes yet they fit tightly on them. The hood didn't even completely cover the person's head, allowing a few strands of blonde hair to peak out from underneath it, and from that alone, I knew exactly who it was before he even spoke.

"Hello again, my elskan..."

It was Calder.

Going On the Run

I gasped as he removed the hood of his black jacket, looking into my eyes with those piercing blue-green eyes of his that had me wanting to drop to my knees in front of him. I don't know why I even tried to tell myself such delusions of ever getting over him if just hearing and seeing him affected me so much.

"Elskan, I've missed you," he continued on as he began to walk toward me. But I quickly began to stumble backward, not wanting him to get too close to me. No matter how much I had missed him, I couldn't let myself fall back into his trap. Not after what he said. Also, let's not forget that he shouldn't even be here in the first place, but back in the Penitentiary.

"W-What are you doing here?" I asked nervously as I clenched my hands into fists to try and ground myself in a way.

"I came for you. I missed you and I wanted to talk with you," he said lowly, smiling a blinding white smile at me that had my heart stuttering in my chest.

"I told you I didn't want to talk to you. I told you to leave me alone," I said, attempting to keep my voice firm, though even I could hear the slight tremor in it.

"And I can't do that. I don't know how many times I've told you or have to tell you that you're mine, elskan," he said, his voice stern and adamant.

"No, no no! Stay away from me!" I said, shaking my head back and forth rapidly as I continued to hurriedly backpedal in a desperate attempt to put more space between us. I couldn't let myself get sucked back in again.

"No, elskan. Not until you let me talk to you and explain myself," he said urgently, a spark of pain shining in his eyes that caught me off guard. But I had to stay firm.

"You shouldn't be here right now, You're supposed to still be in the fucking Penitentiary!" I said in disbelief.

"Yeah, but I heard you quit while I was in isolation. You didn't even give me a chance to explain myself and apologize for being a dumbass!"

At the mention of him apologizing to me, I paused and looked up at him in confusion. I didn't know what or why he was apologizing for.

"Why do you need to apologize to me?" I asked with a furrowed brow.

"Because that day you threw me to the guards in isolation and left me a month ago, I realized what I had done wrong. I know what I had said that had caused everything to go so wrong, so fast," he said, taking a few steps closer before suddenly dropping down to his knees in front of me and looking up at me.

"Calder..." I said in surprise as I looked down at him.

"No, please, just wait a minute. Let me talk to you, and you don't have to say anything. All I ask is that you listen to what I have to say...please?" He begged. I had never heard him sound so, so...desperate and pitiful. It was so unlike him that I felt that I had to hear him out on whatever he was going to say.

"Okay, fine. But can you get up off of your knees and just come sit beside me on the couch? I don't like you being on your knees in front of me. It makes me feel, I don't know, weird," I said uncomfortably.

He quickly stood up and followed me over to the couch. We both sat on opposite ends, just staring at each other for a few moments as we shifted in place. Only once we were situated, shifting having died down to slight hand twitches, did he begin to speak quickly.

"I was wrong, Darby. I was so wrong to make you think that I only wanted you as a plaything or something like that because I don't want you as a plaything. I realized this when I was sitting by myself, locked inside of that tiny ass isolation cell. I need you to be a constant in my life, and I want you and I to be more than just fuck buddies. I want us to have something real together. I want you to be mine for real, Darby," he said with a passion I never expected to hear come from him outside of the more intimate times that we had shared. But I was in shock by his words. I wasn't prepared for him to say that he wanted to have a true relationship and be together for real. Not after what I had been thinking for so long.

"Calder, I don't...I honestly have no idea what to say to that."

"Say you'll give us a chance at having a real relationship. Say that you'll try," he said as he reached across the couch and grabbed both of my hands in his, looking at me with hope and desire.

"Calder, I really want to give us a shot, but I-" I was cut off by loud, urgent banging on my front door that had us both shooting up to our feet and looking at the door cautiously. But I knew better than to stand idle as I quickly jumped into motion. "Go to my bedroom and hide in there until I give you the all-clear."

"There's no way in hell that I'm letting you face whoever's on the other side of that door alone!" He refused instantly.

"Calder, I can handle it! Now, go!" I hissed at him as I went to push him away, but he moved quickly. He leaned into me and pressed his lips to mine, moving our lips in an urgent kiss that had my toes curling against the floor before he pulled back much too soon for my liking. I didn't have time to truly enjoy his lips that I had been missing since I still needed to get the door that was being banged on.

"Be safe, and I'm coming out if I feel like I need to!" He said in a hard voice that left no room for argument.

All I did was nod at him, unable to get anything else out at the moment, before we both separated. I hurried over to the door, opened it, and almost punched the idiot on the other side in the face as I let out a breath of relief. I pulled him inside, closing and locking the door behind him.

"Calder, it's just Sven!" I called out to him resulting in him emerging seconds later as he hurried back over to me.

"FUCK! You almost gave us a heart attack, Sven!" Calder spat angrily at the scared man.

"I'm sorry, but you need to leave. Both of you would probably be best," Sven said hurriedly as he shifted about nervously.

"Both of us? Why do I need to go too?" I asked.

"I got a call from one of our connections back at the Penitentiary. They found footage of the two of you making out in a hallway, and of you both going in and out of Calder's cell," Sven explained.

"Fuck!" I cursed.

"Elskan, calm down and go pack a bag. Grab whatever you find important and take it with you because I'm not leaving you when cops are coming after you for being with me," Calder said. It's not like I had much of a choice in the matter. Besides, he had come back into my life, asking for the chance at something real, showing me that perhaps there was a chance that we could make things work, despite all odds. And I'll be damned if I didn't make sure to try and keep him here by my side with me.

"Okay," I said as I turned and ran to my bedroom where I started throwing some clothes, toiletries, and the few pictures of my family that I had, in a bag. Once done, I rushed back out to where I had left both of them, nodding to let them know I was good.

"You have everything you need?" Calder asked, just to make sure.

"Yeah. What am I going to do with all of my other things though? Like the rest of my clothes, my car, and the apartment?" I questioned.

"Once we get far enough away, we can sell it," Calder said, making me more confused.

"Where am I supposed to live, though?"

"With me," he said without an ounce of hesitation. I looked at him in surprise, getting ready to question that when Sven spoke up after having been looking at his phone.

"Guys, we have to go now. The police, including SWAT, are about ten minutes out," Sven relayed to us.

"Shit. Darby, do you have a hoodie or a jacket or something?" Calder asked.

"Yeah, right here. Why?" I asked, nodding at the hoodie that I had slung over the back of a nearby chair from my shift at the bar the previous night. At least I won't have to go back there again.

"Put it on so that it'll cover your face, and let's get moving," Calder said.

I quickly pulled it on, and then the three of us left, hurrying out of my - now-old - apartment, and then downstairs. We headed straight over to a black SUV that was parked nearby, Sven hopping into the driver's seat while Calder and I got into the back, just barely managing to close the doors before Sven drove off. It was just in time too, because as we were driving off down the street, I saw a bunch of cop cars with sirens blaring, racing off in the direction we'd just come from, the SWAT truck following close behind them.

"Looks like we barely got out of there," Sven noted, sounding relieved.

"No kidding," I said quietly.

Starting Anew...Together

We were driving down some road, the car completely silent as we were all too caught up in our thoughts. The fact that if we hadn't moved as fast as we did, we would have all been caught and arrested for helping a convicted felon to escape (Sven), having escaped from the Penitentiary (Calder), and harboring a convicted felon who had just escaped from the Penitentiary (me), weighing heavy on our minds, though I'm sure, in different ways.

I couldn't believe that all of that had just happened in the span of, maybe two hours. It was probably closer to an hour and a half though because it all just happened so fast.

But now, I was on the run with Calder, and the threat of me possibly, maybe even very likely, getting arrested for being accused - and convicted - of helping him to escape, harboring him, if only for a while after he had just escaped, and then having security footage of the two of us being seen making out and going in and out of his cell while in the Penitentiary. But none of that mattered, and it was the last thing on my mind right now. What was it that was on my mind right now?

It was Calder's earlier words that he had said right before Sven had interrupted us to let us know that we needed to move fast.

He wanted us to have something real, and honestly, so did I. But I couldn't help but fear that this was all just a ploy to make me stay with him so that he could fuck me whenever he wanted. Plus, I had no idea how his family or mine would react to us being together since we've both only been with girls our entire lives. Being with a man instead was way different, and I worried about their responses. I would hate to lose my family, and I doubt he would want to lose his family either.

I felt a hand touch mine that I had resting on my thigh, making me turn to see Calder looking at me with a soft smile on his lips and slight worry in his eyes. God, his smile made him look even more handsome than he already was.

"Hey," Calder said quietly.

"Hey," I said back.

"How are you, you know, doing? With everything that just happened and is going on?" Calder asked me a bit hesitantly, to which I shrugged.

"Fine, I guess. I'm not exactly sure how I should be feeling right now. Should I feel terrified that I could get arrested? Exhilarated from basically running from the cops? How should I feel? Because I'm really not sure right now," I said as I looked at him. I was enjoying the feeling of his large, warm hand on mine as his thumb gently rubbed circles on it for a bit before he threaded our fingers together, giving my hand a reassuring squeeze.

"I don't know, Darby. I don't know how you should feel about all of this. But I do know that even though I'm going to sound like a selfish bastard for saying this, I'm glad that I pulled you into this and got you involved. I like being with you more than I've ever liked being with anyone else. Hell, more than half of the time I spend with Bo and Gunnar I want to either choke or punch them because they get on my nerves. But with you, I just want to spend more time with you. I don't want you to go. I want you to stay by my side," he said, sounding more earnest than I had ever heard him.

I gave him a smile and I found myself leaning in close to him as he leaned into me. Our lips met in the middle, melting together as we held each other close, letting our lips and tongues move slowly against one another. Savoring the feeling of being united like this once more.

"Sorry to interrupt, but it's time for us to get out," Sven said from the driver's seat.

Calder and I pulled away, my cheeks slightly flushed while Calder smirked lightly at me. I turned to see that we were on what appeared to be a private airstrip, a large jet that was black with thin gold stripes beginning at the nose and moving all the way back to its tail, sitting in the middle of the tarmac.

"Why are we getting on a private plane?" I asked as I grabbed my bag, climbing out of the car, all the while staring at the private plane in front of us.

"We have to leave the state to get away from all of the drama and shit," Calder explained as he followed behind me after getting out of the other side of the car.

"Okay, but where are we going then?" I pressed wanting a bit more information, you know, like the actual state that we would be moving to.

"California. Specifically Beverly Hills," Calder said simply.

"Beverly Hills?!" I exclaimed, knowing that typically that is where the rich and famous resided.

"Yeah. That's where Bo and Gunnar already are, as well as my parents," Calder said, making my body lock up as I looked up at him.

"Wait, parents?! I didn't know we were going to your parent's place," I said, feeling my nerves surge. Meeting his parents was never mentioned, never mind living with them!

"We all live together and have for years. Besides, why are you so freaked out about it? You were going to meet them eventually and my dad already knows about you and me since Bo and Gunnar have big mouths," he said with a small huff and roll of his eyes.

"I'm going to kill them," I grumbled as I followed him up the stairs that led to the interior of the plane.

"I'll help you with that, too," Calder said as we finally boarded the plane.

I almost passed out after I looked around at the interior. I'm not sure if luxurious would even work. The color pattern was a mix of black, a few shades of gray ranging from light to dark hues, and creams, giving it a modern look. There was a large, U-shaped couch that took up the entire left side of the plane with a four-foot-long padded rectangular ottoman in the center. Across from the couch were two plush-looking reclining chairs, and then toward the back of the plane I saw a door. There were some additional couches back there with a small coffee table sitting in front of them. Sven had already boarded ahead of us and was stretched out along a couch that was placed in the dead center of the plane.

"Nap time for me," Sven sighed as he wiggled around on the couch to get comfortable before quickly falling asleep. I envy his ability to knock out so fast as I could only dream about that as of late.

"You want to finish our conversation from earlier in the bedroom in the back of the plane?" Calder asked, ignoring Sven entirely to focus on me.

Why I was surprised that there was a bedroom on here was beyond me after seeing everything else the jet had to offer. But I did want to continue our earlier conversation to try and get some more clarification on everything regarding us and our new situation.

"Okay, that would probably be for the best," I agreed, and we headed to the bedroom at the back of the plane, which is what was behind the door I had seen.

We stopped our trek when a stewardess on the jet came up to let us know that we would be taking off, which he thanked her for before Calder continued to guide me back into the bedroom that was bigger than my bedroom back in my old apartment.

The bedroom had similar color patterns to those found in the main area of the plane, with the bed being predominantly a cream color with a black bedspread and a mix of black and cream pillows on the bed. There was also a cream-colored leather recliner placed in the corner on the back wall, a black pillow sitting on the seat, and a desk placed along the wall in front of the recliner.

We sat down on the bed and waited in silence for the plane to get airborne, and I was half tempted to run out to the main area to buckle myself into a seat, but Calder didn't seem concerned. Once we were in the air, we looked at each other and I finally broke the tense silence, jumping right into my worries.

"How do I know that you're not just wanting me to be a steady, but temporary fuck? That you'll only want me until something or someone better comes along where you'll just drop me like a hot potato?" I asked, chewing on my bottom lip anxiously.

"Because I know that there isn't anyone better for me than you. Even if you don't know it yet, you have power over me that I can't understand.

You could tell me to do anything and I'd do it without hesitation," he said, making me raise an amused eyebrow at him as he scooted closer to me, taking hold of both of my hands in his as he stared heatedly into my eyes.

"Anything?" I asked, watching him as he mulled it over in his head.

"Well...anything within reason," he said, amending his previous statement.

"Can I get an example of what something not within reason would be?" I asked with a grin, and he didn't even hesitate with his answer.

"If you tell me to fuck off and that you don't want to be with me, because we both know that not only is that a lie, but that I won't leave you or let you leave me," he said, his eyes darkening.

"Okay, I should have known you would've said that," I chuckled at him.

He scooted impossibly closer to me on the bed before pushing me onto my back, hovering over me as he stared down at me with his bright, mischievous blue-green eyes.

"So, what do you say? Will you agree to finally be mine? To give us a shot?" He asked.

Biting my bottom lip, I looked up at him watching his eyes immediately follow the movement. I let us sit in charged silence for a few seconds more before I finally gave him my answer as I smiled at him.

"Okay. I'll give us a chance," I agreed, pulling him even closer to me, my lips brushing against his as I told him my response.

He grinned and then he leaned down and connected our lips, leaving me with a happy feeling that everything might just work out and be okay between us.

Parent Petrification

Calder and I remained in the bedroom for the duration of the relatively quick flight. Both of us were knotted up together on the bed as we kissed each other like we were making up for lost time because, in a sense, we were. An entire month to be precise.

The jet had just landed but I wanted it to go right back up into the sky. I was not looking forward to meeting his parents, especially not so soon. We only just got together and fixed things, so I was damn scared of adding the pressure of meeting his parents onto our new relationship.

"Come on, it's time to get off," Calder, said, gently nudging me as he sat up from the bed, leaving me to pout up at him from where I remained laying down.

"No, I don't want to."

"Darby, everything will be fine. I don't know why you're freaking out so much," Calder said as he reached down and hauled me up to my feet, pulling me out of the bedroom behind him. I looked at him as if he had gone certifiably insane, and I honestly think that he might have. Why wouldn't I be petrified over something so important?!

"Um, maybe because I, a previously straight male, turned you, their son, a previously straight male, gay! And now we're actually together! They'll probably shoot me!" I exclaimed in a panic as I forced us to stop in the middle of the jet.

Sven, who was now wide awake, came over and picked up my bag that was sitting near the door to exit the jet where I had left it once we had first boarded.

"Meet you two out in the car?" He asked, tossing my bag over his left shoulder.

"Yeah, we're right behind you," Calder said.

"What? No, we're not, because I'm not go-HEY! Put me down, Calder!" I shouted at him, trying to wiggle out of his iron grip which proved to be useless. But I wasn't going down without a fight as I pounded on his back and tried every maneuver I could think of to escape him and his hold.

"No. You're being difficult and we need to go, so honestly, you forced my hand here," he said as exited the jet behind Sven. They both headed over to a large black SUV that was parked and waiting nearby. After Sven placed my bag in the far back of the car and climbed into the driver's seat, Calder deposited me in the back seat, climbing in after me and sitting next to me, wrapping his arms around me to keep me from jumping out of the opposite side's door.

"Just saying, when I die, I'm coming back to haunt your ass for being the reason your parents killed me," I told him grumpily as I crossed my arms over my chest.

Calder rolled his eyes at my dramatics while Sven chuckled as he drove away from the jet, heading toward the house that was going to be my new home, wherever that was. Beverly Hills was a large place, so who knows in what exact area of it we would be staying in.

I sat close to Calder and was unable to stop myself from thinking that I was definitely the more feminine one in our relationship. That was probably a given after I let him fuck my ass, but I also couldn't help but want to always run my hands all over him just so I could stay close to him. I know that if I did, he wouldn't give a fuck and would take great enjoyment in it, the thought making me chuckle softly. Calder turned to look at me with his eyebrow raised and a soft smile on the edge of his lips.

"What's going on up in that head of yours that's got you laughing?" Calder asked.

"Just thinking about how I'm WAY more feminine than you if you know what I mean. Like in our relationship-wise," I said, trying to clarify what I meant, but by the smirk that covered his lips, he completely understood.

"Yeah, you are. I mean, I did fuck you and you loved it and were begging for more," he said cockily. I blushed and turned my red face away from him at his blunt words which had him chuckling.

"I already know that, but thanks for the reminder," I mumbled as I moved to scoot away from him. But his arms encircled my waist, pulling me right back into him and tucking me back into his side, where he wrapped his arms around my shoulders.

"I don't know where you think you're going, but wherever it is, it's not happening. You're going nowhere. You're staying right here with me," he said with a slight, dare I say, pout on his lips.

I couldn't stop the smile that spread across my face as I leaned into his embrace, resting my head on his shoulder comfortably.

"Maybe I wanted to look out of the window," I said. I didn't, but I wanted to keep messing with him since it was both fun and amusing.

"Look out of the windshield then because I don't want you to leave my side."

I rolled my eyes at his possessiveness, but I couldn't stop the constriction that was happening in my pants as he pulled me even closer to him than before.

"I'm going to have to leave your side at some point, like if I need to take a piss or a shit," I said with a snort.

"I'll still go with you. It's not like I haven't seen your sexy body before," he said as he pressed a few kisses along my neck. I tilted my head to the side some, giving him more access which he accepted, beginning to press kisses all over the exposed skin on my neck.

"Hey, horndogs, we're here so break it up," Sven called back to us from the front, making Calder growl at him.

"Remember who pays you, Jacubsen," Calder said, never removing his lips from my neck.

"What? I'm just stating the truth. You two are on the verge of stripping and fucking back there, and I don't want any part of that," Sven shot back.

My cock pulsed hard with desire as I remembered the last time that Calder and I were both completely naked and how the sex had been so mind-numbingly good. So much so that I found myself wanting it to happen again and again and again.

Calder left one last kiss on my collarbone before pulling away from me. I couldn't stop the whine that escaped my lips at the loss of pleasure, making his head snap back around to me as he smirked at me with lust-filled eyes.

"That was sexy. Do it again," he demanded, his voice low and husky.

"No! I didn't even know I could make that sound!" I cried out as I blushed, making his smirk widen.

"I'm going to make you let out so many different sounds that you've never made before, and I'll enjoy them all," he purred. And then he turned and exited the car like what he had just said was something normal to have been said, leaving me to sit there frozen and blushing. "You coming?" He called back into the car to me, snapping me out of my daze, reminding me of my current predicament, which also brought back my nerves.

"No, you have fun," I said instantly to which he glared at me, reachiing back into the car to grab my legs and pulling me into his chest. He locked his arms around me as I tried to wiggle away from him again."Let me go, Calder!"

"No. Since you're being so difficult, I'm just going to have to carry you," he said as he pulled me fully out of the back of the SUV. He shut the door with his hip before moving his hands down to grab and squeeze my ass, making me jump in surprise which caused both of our cocks to involuntarily rub together, eliciting low moans from both of us.

"C-Calder, stop groping my ass," I panted slightly, unable to keep myself from pressing into his cock more.

"Not happening, elskan," he said as he pecked my cheek followed by a sudden shrill cry erupting behind us, making me jump in surprise.

"My baby! You're finally home and you brought your friend!"

I turned around to see a petite, middle-aged blonde woman scurrying towards us with a massive smile on her face. As she approached, I noticed she had a set of shimmering blue eyes, looking the part of a European woman. She was obviously his mother and was a stunning woman even though she was what some may call 'older'.

I tried to get down from Calder's hold to either run for the hills or not be in such an embarrassing position as I had yet to decide which option was best at the moment. But he just held onto me tighter, preventing me from going anywhere.

"Calder, put me down!" I hissed, but he just smirked at me again.

"Why? So you can run? No thanks, I'm good," he chuckled just as his mother finally made it to us which had Calder grinning at her before greeting her in Icelandic. "Hæ mamma, ég saknaði þín líka."(Hi mother, I missed you too.)

"Don't be rude, Calder! Introduce me to your friend, and speak English since he isn't familiar with our language! I've raised you better than that," She teased him, making him chuckle while she kept her eyes on me. I was still trying to get out of Calder's hold which was useless since he just kept gripping me tighter.

"Of course, mamma. But first, where's Faðir?" Calder had barely gotten the question out when a man, seemingly out of nowhere, appeared next to Calder's mother. He was similar to Calder in that he was tall, easily towering over Calder's mother and me, and he was also tatted up with swirling lines and depictions of some kind of tribal type. But, instead of Calder's blonde hair, his was a dark chocolate brown, and he had a medium-length full beard, though it wasn't unkept in the slightest and was groomed to perfection. He also had a pair of hazel eyes that practically screamed of trouble while also easily capturing the attention of many in a pleasant way. It seemed as though Calder's blue-green eyes had, in a sense, been inherited from both his mother and father.

"Ah, about time you showed up," he said as he looked at Calder before he turned, his eyes locking on me. "You must be the ass that my son's been getting."

Fuck, I think I'm paralyzed with fear.

Grand Tour

"**Y**ou must be the ass that my son is getting," his father said, looking at me with a smirk while I just stared back, unable to move a damn muscle.

"Faðir!" Calder exclaimed in exasperation while his father chuckled, finding his shout funny while I remained frozen in shock.

"I'm just messing around with the two of you," he grinned.

"Well, neither of us appreciates it. Mamma, and Faðir, I would like to introduce you both to Darby Kelby, my boyfriend. Darby, this is my Mamma, Sonya, and my Faðir, Odin," Calder introduced us all to one another proudly. I was waiting for looks of disgust from them, but I was only shown two bright smiles of happiness, yet Calder's father's smile was more on the edge of a smirk. I had a feeling that Odin was the more physically mature version of Calder, and I wasn't sure if I could handle two of them at once.

"So you finally manned up and fucked him then?" His father said, making my eyes go wide as my cheeks flared a bright red at his father's words. Yeah, these two are definitely alike and are sure to keep me blushing.

"Odin!"

"Faðir!"

Both Calder and his mother shouted at his father in exasperation.

"What? Was I wrong?" His father, Odin, asked as he looked between the two of us, my cheeks going darker as Calder scowled.

"You're not wrong, Odin, they fucked," Gunnar's voice suddenly spoke, soon followed after by Bo's.

"Yeah, and then they fought and now apparently they're dating," Bo spoke next, always needed to throw in his two cents, whether they were wanted or not.

Calder growled at them while I frowned and looked away as we both recalled our fight. It was more of a misunderstanding though, yet it all led up to all the shit storm that is currently going down.

"Well, you can look at everything in a positive way," his mother said as she looked at Calder and me, my arms locked around his neck as I rested comfortably on his hip, looking up at her with a small frown on my lips.

"How, mamma?! That is not something that either of us would like to think about!" Calder huffed out.

"Maybe so, but you two are now together. As boyfriends. Tell me, if that little fight you two had didn't happen, would you two be together as you now are?" She asked knowingly.

Calder turned to look at me with a raised brow that had me chuckling.

"No, probably not. But if Calder had his way, then yeah, we would be," I said.

"If I had my way, we would have already fucked more than just the one time that we did," he said, always having to turn things sexual. My cheeks flared at his words and the way his eyes darkened. With a final, stronger jerk, I managed to finally escape his tight hold on me as I walked over to Sven who was standing off to the side, holding my bag that he had gotten out of the SUV for me.

"Can you take me to the room I'll be staying in, please? I'm tired," I asked.

"Yeah, sure," he agreed as he went to lead me off when Calder cut off his path.

"No, I'll do it. You'll be staying in my room with me, elskan," he said as he took my hand in his. I took my bag from Sven when I passed him as Calder started to tow me behind him by our intertwined hands, but I stopped him and looked at him in disagreement.

"I am not sharing a room with you," I refused.

"Why not? We've already shared a bed," he winked at me, smirking, resulting in me glaring at him.

"No, Calder. Not happening," I said adamantly.

"It is too. You can fight it all you want, but I'm just telling you what's going to be happening," he said matter of factly, and damn if I didn't know that he was telling the truth. He was one stubborn bastard.

"Fine...you fucking pain in the ass," I grumbled, mumbling out the last part.

A swift smack landed across my ass, making it obvious that he had heard me. He admitted as much a moment later.

"I heard that, and if anything, you like the pain in your ass that I give you. Now, let's head into the house and up to our room. I'll give you a tour on the way."

With red-stained cheeks, we walked the rest of the way up to the house that I previously hadn't paid much attention to. But looking at it now, I couldn't deny that it was both gorgeous and massive.

The large mansion was painted a bright, pristine white and was topped with a plain black tiled roof. I could see at least three chimneys from my view, but I was sure that there was more based on the place's sheer size. It looked as though it was a luxurious hotel from the front and the way that there were at least fifteen steps up before stepping under a large, clear glass overhang that doubled as a small porch, leading to the massive glass double doors with vines made from iron running across it. I even noticed the same vine pattern on some of the lower windows that spanned out across the first floor, and on the four balconies on the second floor that were visible from the front. To the right of the mansion, I saw a single floored room of some sort that was built almost at an angle to the rest of the house, but it was still attached to the main portion. I was curious to know what it was on the inside.

Calder opened the front door, having me enter inside first before following behind me, though our hands were still linked together since we had never separated.

The entryway was a stunning, shining white marble with two twin, solid white marble staircases, the railings on each also containing the iron vine-pattern woven through it, and two large mirrors covering up a large portion of either side of the walls next to the staircases. At the apex of the easily, at least thirty-foot tall room hung a large crystal chandelier from an even larger skylight. The light from the sky and chandelier reflected off of the hanging crystals making it appear to sparkle, as well as everything else in the entryway.

Everything here was such a clean and pristine white that I was afraid to move for fear of scuffing up the marble floors in some way, but I was forced to proceed when Calder began walking forward, leaving me no choice but to follow after him.

"I'll show you everything downstairs first, and then we'll head upstairs and to our room," he explained to which I let out a little huff.

"Correction, YOUR room. I let the first one slip," I told him.

"No, our room. We're sharing it from now on," he said, making me roll my eyes.

"How long do you expect me to stay here?" I asked.

"Seeing as how myself, Gunnar, and Bo are wanted for escaping from the Penitentiary, and consequently you are too from our involvement together at the Penitentiary that they know about, I'm going to have to say ab out...forever," he said, continuing to guide me forward as he began the tour. Meanwhile, I was shocked by his words, realizing the gravity of our situation, yet I remained silent for the time being. I wanted to just remain in blissful ignorance for the time being.

"This is the main sitting area," he said as we walked through a large white-painted room with lightly colored, shining wood flooring, and had a fireplace with a TV mounted on the wall above it, with four, navy blue tufted couches spaced out in a rectangle with two on each side of a long, lightly colored Persian rug with two glass and gold coffee tables sitting in between the two sets of couches that faced one another, a chandelier hung above each coffee table.

From there, we proceeded to a second sitting room that was off to the left of the previous one. This one was smaller but was also white with a fireplace and mounted TV with four, white two-seater loveseats in the center of the glossy, light wood floors in a square shape, another matching chandelier centered above them, and two sets of French doors, one to close this area off from the previous, and another leading to what appeared to be a backyard. I also noticed that in the back right corner near the back doors, there was a mirrored wall with a white, octagon pattern made into it with a decently sized bar setup, including three black, mid-backed stools, a tall bartop with two built-in taps, and a large-mirrored liquor cabinet on the back wall.

We went to the next room which was the kitchen with another attached sitting area with another fireplace and TV. The combined area had dark wooden cabinets and more pristine, white marble for all of the countertops in the kitchen, and the accent wall where the fireplace was. There was a window over top of the sink that looked out into the backyard, a large black gas-range stove and oven, a massive matching black refrigerator, and a long dark wood island in the middle with an even larger, almost wrap-around counter a few feet in front that essentially acted as a divider between the kitchen and where the black, leather couches were arranged in a U-shape. Again, there were two more chandeliers, each centered over each area to make them look not as conjoined, which I felt worked well, especially since the wood floors seemed to continue throughout the house, even continuing into the dining room alongside the kitchen.

The dining room was large and ornate, just like everything else I had seen thus far. The ceilings were high with two chandeliers spaced out over the top of the long dark wood dining room table with more dark wood, and white upholstered chairs than I currently felt like counting. Two more sets of double French doors also doubled as large windows that let in lots of light from the backyard, and thick cream-colored curtains pulled back to let the light in. I also clocked another fireplace as well in here.

We then went across the way to yet another sitting area that he explained was mainly used as a waiting area for when he has people come over for 'business', whatever all that entails. I noticed that this area was the room I'd seen from the front that was positioned differently from the rest of the house. The room itself was dome-shaped with a skylight in the center of the ceiling with another chandelier hanging from it, this chandelier hanging lower as it was larger than the others. There were two large, curved, cream-greyish colored modular sectional sofas sitting across from each other, an ottoman in front of each as they were placed in front of another fireplace. Off in a side room to the waiting area was a large bar that took up the whole room, having two dark-wood bar tops in two of the corners, with two of the walls covered in dark wooden cabinets that held liquors of various types.

He then led me down another hallway where his office was - it was made from all dark wood starting with the desk and a black plush chair for him with two small cream-colored chairs on the other side for guests, walls, ceiling with a small yet elegant chandelier, the bookcases that were built into the wall, and the French doors leading into the room as well as the two, separate, double French doors that lead out into the back yard. The darkness of his office was something I found soothing and rustic, and I thought it suited him and his tastes well.

After his office, he brought me to a theater room with a large movie screen and eight large, comfortable-looking reclining chairs. The room looked like a small version of a public movie theater, and then he showed me a nearby indoor pool after that. The pool was something else as it reminded me of something that would be found up in Olympus with the Greek Gods and Goddesses but it also looked like it was right out of a Versace magazine or TV ad. It was kind of hard to describe, but I definitely thought that a Versace emblem should be located inside it somewhere.

The entire mansion was just absolutely magnificent and unreal. And to think, we were only just on the first floor!

"Your place is amazing, Calder. I'm definitely putting that indoor pool to use some time while I'm here if you don't mind," I said, still thinking about the pool even after we had left it, having circled around to a back staircase and walking up it together.

"Of course, I don't mind. Since we're heading upstairs, and I can see how tired you are, I'm going to spare you from seeing most of it as it's mainly just bedrooms, but as you can see now that we're at the top, there's a sitting room here, too," Calder explained.

And sure enough, there was another sitting room with two single leather chairs on one side, a large white leather couch on the other, and a coffee table in between. There was also another chandelier in the middle, and a fireplace as well which was built into a wooden wall with storage cabinets on either side.

"You and your family sure like having sitting rooms, chandeliers, and fireplaces. Wasn't there like six sitting rooms with fireplaces in each, and a chandelier in every room?" I asked him teasingly.

"Very funny. But there are only actually five sitting rooms, and seven fireplaces, and the indoor pool, smaller and larger bar, and movie theater are the only rooms without chandeliers. But let's not spend too much time on that and let's head to our room," he said. Had it not been for the fact that I was tired and ready to sleep, I would've been awed at the fact that he knew the exact numbers to everything, and also corrected him for calling the room 'ours' again. But I just let it all slip past.

He walked us down the hallway and to the door located at the very end of it, pushing it open when we reached it.

"Holy...fuck," I managed to get out as I looked around the room in awe.

It also looked like something from a Versace commercial, or something Mediterranean or Greek with how extraordinary it was. The room consisted of mainly white colors with gold accents everywhere, including on the large overhead chandelier. The large bed placed against the far left wall was encased in a large, indoor gazebo-esque area made out of cement. Four columns were holding it up with about two-and-a-half to three-foot small concrete pillars that wrapped almost all the way around the bed, enclosing it except for small gaps on either side that allowed for people to easily walk through. The bed itself was also massive, the sheets of the bed being mainly maroon in color, with gold accents being the darkest thing in the otherwise bright room. There were also large, picturesque windows spanning the entire side of the room, as the room itself was round. It was just absolutely amazing. It looked like a room fit for a royal prince or king or something.

"Like it?" Calder asked.

"This room is so...it's just...fuck!" I managed to splutter out in my awe-induced state.

He laughed as he led me in further to shut the door, and then took my bag from my hand and tossed it to the side.

"Since you are apparently in shock, I'm undressing you," he said as he quickly pulled off my sweater shirt, making me snap out of my daze as I gave him a sharp look.

"What are you doing?"

"I'm taking off your clothes so that we can both get in bed and go to sleep. We can shower in the morning," he explained. I nodded my head as I kicked off my shoes and pulled off my shorts, leaving me in just my boxers.

"Alright sounds good because I'm fucking exhausted."

"I can't wait to actually sleep on a damn bed that's worth something instead of that stupid shitty bed that they have at the Penitentiary," Calder sighed happily. I chuckled as I turned to look back at Calder after having been looking at the bed wantonly. When I looked at Calder, I was blessed with a damn good sight.

I felt my entire body temperature rise as I stared at him as he leaned against the small table near him, sporting only his tight black briefs. If it wasn't for the fact that my mouth had gone dry at the sight of how good he looked, I would have been salivating. It also didn't help that his eyes were slowly running over my body.

"You okay over there, elskan?" He asked me with a smirk while all I could do was stare at him and give a small, dumb nod. "Okay, let's get some sleep."

"Mhm," was all I could muster out as I quickly climbed into the bed, loving how it felt like I was sinking some before it firmed up and melded to the shape of my body. I hummed in delight as Calder got in the bed, laying down beside me with a smile.

"Night, elskan. Sleep well," he said as he immediately pulled me into his embrace, resting his head atop mine. I, almost subconsciously, leaned further into his embrace and pressed my face into the crook of his neck, feeling my entire body fully relax for the first time in years.

"Night, Calder," I murmured out before falling asleep in half a second, maybe even less. Maybe it wasn't so difficult for me to knock out like Sven had on the jet. All I needed was Calder by my side.

Morning Wake Up Call

I was completely knocked out, enjoying my dead sleep when I stirred at a pair of hands slowly running along my sides and torso. I could also hear a quiet voice saying something, but I fought to ignore it, wanting nothing more than to continue my amazing sleep. But the soft voice and moving hands were persistent in their wandering. And when I say wandering, I do mean WANDERING.

I felt the hands move down my body slowly as they lightly played with the waistband of my boxers. They were pulling the band back some before releasing it, letting it slap back in place against my body a few times before a hand slipped below the waistband and into my boxers, wrapping around my straining morning wood. The hand stroked me slowly, making me squirm and moan lightly. As the stroking movement continued, a set of lips began to place kisses all over my neck, sucking lightly at the skin on my neck.

I wasn't stupid. I knew who was kissing and stroking me, so I just let Calder do it some before I slowly opened my eyes. I blinked a few times to wake myself up, seeing Calder staring at me as he continued kissing along my neck and collarbone.

"I was...mmm...trying to sleep, Havard," I rasped out, letting out a small moan.

"Oh? We're back to my last name again?" He raised an eyebrow before etching his lips from my neck and moving them up to brush against mine as he spoke huskily to me.

"Yes because I'm trying to sleep and you're groping me," I huffed out, though I wasn't completely bothered.

"Maybe, but I know that you're enjoying it, Kelby," Calder responded knowingly, and I shuddered as he said my last name, speeding up his motions on my cock, tightening his grip as well.

"Shit, I'm going to cum," I groaned quietly when he began pumping faster. He dropped his head back down to my neck, sucking at my skin and leaving love bites behind, no doubt.

Just as I was about to release, the bedroom door swung open, both Bo and Gunnar strolling in like they owned the place.

"Morning," Gunnar grinned.

"What are you two up to?" Bo asked.

An instant boner killer.

I. Am. Pissed.

"Don't you two bastards know how to fucking knock?!" Calder shouted angrily while I burrowed down into the sheets and comforter that covered us. I buried my face in his throat to hide my red face that was burning with a mix of embarrassment and anger.

"You know we don't," Gunnar snorted.

"Besides, it's not like you two were busy anyway," Bo said with a shrug as if he knew everything.

I moved my hand up to grip Calder's bicep to keep from exploding at the two dumbasses that were standing at the foot of the bed, and I don't mean in the good way that would be a result of my release. No, I was feeling murderous right now.

"Yeah, actually, we are," Calder said gruffly, giving my cock, which was still in his hand, a firm squeeze that had my head tossing backward, letting out a loud, hungry moan.

"Mmm...fuck."

I knew he did that to prove his point to the two idiots whose eyes went wide upon realizing that we actually were busy. I was too horny to even be embarrassed by the fact that I had been so loud and obvious in front of Bo and Gunnar.

"Oh, fuck! Are you dick deep in his ass?!" Gunnar gasped out.

"No, but if you two fucks hadn't come in, there was a good possibility that I could have been! Plus, I'm always balls deep, not dick deep."

I was too focused on Calder's hand that was wrapped around my dick to give a fuck about what they were talking about, or even comprehend it. All I knew was that I was once again, painfully hard and desperate to have Calder's cock shoved up my ass. And I'd be damned if I didn't get it within the next five minutes since there was no way in hell I was letting him go in me without some sort of lubricant since I didn't feel like having my ass ripped open at the moment. Maybe later though.

I finally managed to find my voice to get these three to shut the fuck up so I could get what I wanted.

"Will you three shut the fuck up already?! Bo and Gunnar get the fuck out! And Calder, find some fucking lube and a condom! Now!" I shouted.

I watched as Bo and Gunnar's eyes practically popped out of their sockets at my demands. Calder let go of my cock, making me whimper for a moment at the loss of contact, as he shot out of the bed to hurriedly get both of the things I had requested of him.

"So, we're just going to leave now," Bo said.

"Good, now go!"

They both turned and ran out of the room, but before closing the door, Gunnar poked his head back in for a second more.

"Have fun and try not to be too loud!" He said, causing both Calder and I to shout at them at the same time.

"Fuck off!"

With laughs from Bo and Gunnar, they shut the door, finally leaving. They did so at the right time too because Calder came hurrying back over to me, his briefs already off leaving him hard and naked as he quickly climbed up the bed. He ripped the comforter and sheets from my body once he reached me, his hands moving down to grab the waistband of my boxers. He pulled them off, chucking them behind him as he leaned over top of me, connecting our lips in a frenzied, needy kiss.

I locked my arms around his neck and my legs around his waist, lifting my hips off of the bed. I rubbed both of our bare erections against each other's, moaning into one another's mouths as our lips remained locked in a passionate kiss. Calder's hands wandered down to grab a hold of my ass, giving it a firm squeeze, eliciting another moan from me before he pulled his lips away, leaving us both panting.

"Now, it's time to prep you so that I can have that ass wrapped around my cock again," he panted, not hesitating to slide down my body until he was settled in between my legs.

He spread my legs with one hand while the other moved to open the small bottle of lube, applying it to my twitching hole rapidly. His fingers pushed inside of me, working me quickly so that I was stretched enough to be able to take him in.

"Calder, at this point I don't give a fuck if it hurts or not! Just fucking fuck me already!" I cried out desperately, ignoring my previous thought of wanting to be lubed and everything else.

"Don't have to tell me twice," he said as he quickly opened the condom, sliding it onto his shaft.

I spread my legs as wide as possible, reaching down to fist the bed sheet in preparation for what I knew would be a hard and fast entry into my ass. And I wasn't wrong when his hips quickly shot forward as he thrusted into me with one powerful thrust that had my back arching. An ear-splitting scream that was a mixture of both pain and pleasure ripped from my throat.

"AGGGHHH! CALDER!"

Calder let out a happy, pleasured moan as he buried himself fully within me, his hands moving to my hips where he gripped them tightly. He began to drill into me, hitting my prostate with each thrust, not even giving me a chance to adjust to his size as he continued to ram into me. I screamed with each thrust as the pleasure masked any of the initial pain that I was feeling.

"Fuck! You feel so fucking good! Fuck!" He screamed as he continued to pound into me as I arched my back off of the bed.

I'm pretty sure that ever since he first thrust into me, my back has yet to touch the bed. And I was perfectly okay with that since it felt like he was getting deeper with every thrust inside of me. I could feel the muscles in my stomach tighten as my toes curled, signaling that I was getting close, very close, to my peak.

"CALDER! I'm close!" I shrieked to which he responded with a grunt.

"Fuck, me too! Ungh, cum NOW, elskan!" He yelled as he buried himself deeper than before, releasing into the condom while my cock twitched wildly, spraying cum between both of our sweaty bodies.

He slowly pulled out of me a few minutes later, making me grunt. He stood up as he removed the used condom, tying it off at the end and looking down at me with his eyes slowly raking across my body.

"What?" I asked through a slight pant.

"Want to join me in the shower?"

"I would, but my ass is so fucking sore that I'm not sure if I can get up from the bed, or even sit up for that matter," I said as my cheeks went a little rosy.

"Well, I'll just carry you then," he said with a grin. He then leaned down, scooping up my exhausted and sweaty body in a bridal carry as he walked us into the massive ensuite bathroom, tossing the used condom he still held into a nearby trash can upon entry to the bathroom.

The bathroom was almost as big as my bedroom and the main living area in my old apartment, combined. The entire right wall, upon immediate entry to the bathroom, was nothing but a large mirror on the top half of the wall while the lower half was all lighter-colored wooden cabinetry for the massive dual sink vanity. The fixtures were a shining silver with small yet bright, tasteful lights built into the wall over the large vanity, and a large tufted silvery-grey ottoman in the dead center of the bathroom, situated underneath a skylight that took up nearly the entire ceiling in the bathroom. To the left of the door we had just entered was a large vanity with a table with some bottles of cologne and other things scattered across the top, a chair, and a large circular mirror with a candelabra-esque light fixture on one side of it. Just on the other side of the vanity was another door that was open, and I could see that it led into an entire other room- I mean a closet. The closet looked like a high-end men's fashion store from my vantage point in his arms.

On the opposite wall was a large glass shower that took up three-quarters of the far left wall, with tan marble accents, and a bench seat in it. The last quarter or so of the wall looked like a built-in sauna or something like that, and in front of the sauna was a big jacuzzi bathtub that was also surrounded by tan marble with the same built-in cabinets as was found in the vanity The tub was situated in front of a bay window that took up three-quarters of the height of the wall, and next to that was another smaller vanity thing of some sort with a damn forty-five to fifty-inch flat screen TV above it.

"Why in the hell do you have a TV in your bathroom?" I asked, eying the mounted TV up in the corner, straight across from us. He chuckled softly as he walked over to the shower, turning it on and letting the water begin heating up before we got in.

"The real question is why don't you have a TV in your bathroom?" He joked back.

"Um, because I'm poor!" I said, giving him an incredulous look that had him chuckling more as he walked us both into the now warmed-up shower. He stood us right underneath the direct, warm spray of water since I was still situated in his arms and didn't have any intention of lowering as of yet.

"Yeah, that was before. But now you don't have to ever worry about any-thing ever again because I'm going to take care of you," he said seriously, leaning in and pressing a gentle kiss to my lips that had butterflies flying around in my stomach.

Damn, he was turning me into such a girl. And I'd be lying if I said that I gave a shit because I honestly kind of like it. I like the way that he makes me feel.

After our nice, long shower, he dried us both off and then carefully set me down on the ottoman in the center. He then went into the closet, emerging a few short minutes later with clothes for us both in hand before we began to get dressed for the day.

The outfit he chose for me was a pair of cuffed black jeans, a white t-shirt, an open long-sleeved denim button-up shirt with the sleeves rolled up to my elbows, white ankle socks, and plain white low sneakers. I liked it because it was something I would normally wear and was incredibly comfortable, even in my currently pained state.

Calder, on the other hand, was looking fucking delicious. He wore a plain, long-sleeved red shirt with black jeans, the knees ripped on them, white socks, and a pair of bright red high-top sneakers. He topped off his outfit with a large gold wristwatch that he secured on his right hand that just served to make him look hotter.

Calder and I had just finished getting dressed when the ringing of my phone sounded off, and I recalled placing it on the nightstand next to the side of the bed that I had slept on, the night before.

Calder plucked me back up in his arms, having helped me dress due to the ache in my ass, and carried me over to the nightstand, allowing me to pick up my phone. I didn't think much of anything about who could be calling me, expecting it to be a scam call or something to that effect since the only people I talked to anymore were all currently with me in the same house as

I was. So, I didn't even bother glancing at the Caller ID as I answered the call.

"Hello?"

"It's about damn time that you picked up the phone. We need to talk."

Oh, shit. I am so fucked.

A Harrowing Call

My entire body just completely froze at the sound of the voice on the other end of the line. The words seemed to continually bounce around in my skull, my body shaking slightly from how nervous I was from hearing his voice after so long, and the barely concealed anger that was in it.

Calder, who was still carrying and therefore holding me, noticed my change in mood immediately. In an effort to try and calm me down, he tightened his grip on me, pulling me further into his chest so that my head rested over the top of his heart. The combined feeling of one of his hands caressing my spine, paired with hearing the strong, steady thumping of his heart beneath my ear helped to slowly calm me down, though not fully. Just being near him always did wonders for me when I felt like I was spiraling, even when he was the cause.

"Well, are you going to say something?" He said, his voice growing angrier over the line.

"Yeah, sorry Dad. I was just a little bit busy. I just got out of the shower, and I-"

"I don't give a fuck what you were doing, Darby. But I'm going to ask you a question, and I expect an honest answer, got it?" He said sternly, cutting me off, and making me try to hold back a nervous gulp.

"Yes, sir," I said lowly, unable to keep from swallowing nervously. I brought my hand up, which wasn't currently clutching my phone in a death grip, to tightly hold onto one of Calder's large biceps, keeping a firm grip on it to try and ready myself for what his next words would be.

"Your mother and I received a call a few weeks back from your friend, Grant, telling us that you came out to him as gay. Is this, or is this not, true?"

If it weren't for the fact that I was already no longer friends with him, that would have definitely severed any kind of ties I had to Grant. I can't believe that bastard called my parents and told them I was gay before I had the chance to do so myself!

"Yes Dad, it is true. But, before you say anything, I would just like to say that not only are Grant and I no longer friends but also, I don't really care to hear your thoughts on MY sexuality. Who I decide to be in a relationship with, regardless of their gender, is of no concern to you."

I don't know where the fuck that came from, but having said it all was not only kind of liberating, but it also scared the shit out of me to admit all of that. My dad was not someone that you spoke that way to. He expected nothing but respect, and if you didn't give it to him, you were fucked, to say the least.

Before he even said anything, I knew that he was beyond pissed because I could hear his breathing grow marginally heavier from down the line.

"Darby, either you head home now, or we're heading up to your place now. What's it going to be? " He finally said, not even saying anything back in response to my precious words, only serving to make me even more nervous.

"Well, I'm not going back to the house, and I don't live in Vegas anymore, so that's not happening either."

"What the fuck are you talking about?! When the fuck did you move, and why didn't you call and tell me?!" He demanded. I frowned at his words, feeling myself getting angrier at the way he felt the need to tell me what I should do in my own life despite being a full-fledged, legal adult.

"Why are you getting so mad? I'm twenty-three years old. I don't need to tell you what I do, and when I do it! Yeah, you're my dad, but I'm not a kid anymore, so stop treating me like one!" I yelled angrily.

Calder pulled me impossibly closer, planting kisses along my face and then down my neck, seemingly pulling out the big guns to calm me down. And, of course, it was working too, as I moved my head to come to rest on his shoulder, leaning my head back to look up at him and then leaning in to press a kiss to his jawline that had him smiling at me softly. He looked like a contented puppy that had just been rewarded for successfully sitting on command for the first time.

"Maybe not, but you are my son. Therefore, I have every right to know your whereabouts at all times. Now, either you tell me where you are and why, or I find out on my own, and I doubt you want that to happen," he threatened.

Again, my body went stiff because he knew that was the last thing that I wanted.

"I'm in California, and I moved to have a fresh start away from everyone and everything," I said, giving in with a sigh.

"Where in California, and who are you with? I can hear someone else's breathing as well as yours."

Damn him and his fucking training.

"Beverly Hills. I moved in with my boyfriend and his family," I said stiffly, knowing I had no way of getting out of this.

"Boyfriend? You already have a boyfriend?"

"Yes."

"What's his name? I want to look into him."

My eyes widened and I began to panic. There is no way in hell that I'm telling him Calder's name, then we'll both end up in prison, more specifically the Penitentiary, again. Though this time we'll both end up being the inmates.

"No, Dad. I'm not telling you that. Look, I have to go. Tell Mom and Elijah I said hi and I love them. I'll talk to you some other time. Bye," I said, not hesitating to quickly hang up the phone, even going so far as to shut it off since I knew he would call back or even potentially track it.

I leaned further into Calder's hold, feeling his lips press a few more kisses to my head as I heaved out a heavy sigh.

"Talk to me, elskan. What was that?" He asked softly.

"As you probably picked up on and understood, that was my dad on the line," I said tiredly.

"Yes, I got that. But what about that has got you so tense?"

"You heard the conversation, I'm sure. But you don't get why I'm so terrified of him," I said as I looked up at him worriedly, not exactly answering him. I was trying to put it off for as long as possible, but that wasn't going to happen because I knew my dad and how crazy he could get in tracking me down so that he could come after me.

"No, not a clue," he agreed.

"Instead of telling everyone a bunch of times, why don't we just go downstairs and see if everyone's around since it will probably affect everyone," I sighed again, begrudgingly.

"Okay then?" He said in confusion, though phrasing it more like a question as he moved to walk off but paused momentarily. "How're you feeling, elskan? I don't just mean after talking with your dad."

"Tired," I admitted. "I'm really damn sore, and talking with my dad just stressed me out, so now all I want to do is sleep because it's all so fucking exhausting. But I can't, not yet at least."

"I understand, elskan. Just relax for a little," he said, giving my thighs, that now both of his hands were holding, a squeeze. I wrapped myself around him like a koala bear, my face buried in his neck as he walked downstairs, a hand having moved to rub my ass while the other one raised to rub my back as I struggled to remain calm and not spiral or panic like I wanted to.

"Hey, the lovebirds emerged!" Gunnar cheered.

"You fuck him to sleep, Calder?" Bo tacked on, making him and Gunnar laugh as I groaned, Calder growling angrily.

"Will you two shut the fuck up?! Where are my parents?" He asked.

"We're right here, why?" I heard Odin say in confusion a moment later.

"What's wrong with Darby?" Sonya asked in concern.

"He's stressed and has something he wants to talk to us all about," Calder clarified somewhat, not knowing too much more than they did.

I finally pulled away from Calder, slowly detaching myself from him and standing on my own two feet. I sighed as I rubbed at my face roughly before looking back at Calder, his parents, Bo and Gunnar, and even Sven who was leaning on a nearby wall. All of them looked at me in concern upon seeing the exhausted look I wore.

"I'm not going to bullshit or sugarcoat anything here, I'm just going to say it: we're all fucked and I've both unintentionally and inadvertently put you all at risk for being thrown back into the Penitentiary."

A Dangerous Realization

C alder frowned in confusion as he looked at me.

"Elskan, what are you talking about? How are we all at risk of going back to the Penitentiary by being with you?" Calder asked me, but I ignored his question in favor of basking in my own inner turmoil.

I felt like shit right now because the only thing that I could think of was that I needed to leave. I had to leave and let my dad know I was gone, and on my own so he would leave them be and come after me. I knew it would suck to have to be away from Calder since I had gone and gotten attached to him. But if it meant keeping him and his family safe, I would do it in a heartbeat and without complaint.

"Elskan, look at me," Calder insisted as he moved to physically pull me out of my thoughts by gently holding my face in his hands. His thumbs softly brushed my cheeks as he looked down at me with more concern than he had ever shown me, having picked up on my brewing inner turmoil. "What are you talking about? Explain it to us."

I sighed as I looked away from him, letting the words roll off of my tongue. The sooner they knew of the danger I posed, the sooner I could get out of their hair and keep them all safe.

"My dad used to work up in the higher level ranks of the FBI, and he will, occasionally, still do some odd jobs for them. When he finds out where I'm at and who I'm with - since there is no if since he will find me - he's going to put you all back into the fucking Penitentiary, beat my ass, and then throw me in there too for treason or some other shit similar to that just to prove a point that he can and will. His son or not," I said, squeezing my eyes shut as I waited for them to start yelling at me, or for Calder to punch me since I did deserve it.

But nothing of that sort happened.

Instead, I felt Calder quickly pull me tightly to his chest, hugging me close as he pressed soft kisses all over the top of my head.

"That won't happen, elskan. We won't let it happen, so don't stress yourself out over it," he said with certainty, prompting me to open my eyes and look up at him.

"But Calder, you don't seem to get it: you're all fucked and it's all my fault," I stressed.

"Darby, just relax. We can handle your father. We aren't going back to the Penitentiary and we won't let you go either," Gunnar said with a scoff.

"Yeah, besides, if he wants to come here, let him. There are more of us than there is of him," Bo said with a cocky grin, but I shook my head insistently.

"No. I can't let him come here. I don't want any of you, or him, to get hurt. I think I should just leave. It will keep y-"

Calder's eyes suddenly filled with fury as he pulled me impossibly closer to his chest, cutting off the rest of what I was trying to say.

"No! Hell fucking no! You aren't going anywhere, Darby! You're staying here with me where you belong, and you're not going to say otherwise, so don't even try it! And I know how you think, so you're not just going to up and leave in the middle of the night! I will fucking chain your ass to our bed!" He growled angrily, which caused a few snickers to be heard from behind us at his words. I turned around, first noting that we were in the kitchen which I had failed to notice earlier, but that it was the two idiots and Sven who had laughed in the first place. It seemed like they were bringing Sven into their dark, childish side.

"That sounds like some kinky shit right there," Sven cackled.

"I know!" Gunnar agreed.

"I was thinking the same damn thing!" Bo said, laughing along with them.

"Being chained up just makes the sex even better, though. Don't you agree, Sonya?" Odin suddenly added in, giving his wife a seductive smirk and wink that had her giggling.

"Faðir! Mamma! I don't want to hear that kind of shit! That's fucking disgusting!" Calder cried out, gagging as he wrinkled his nose in disgust, making his mother roll her eyes at him.

"Please, how the hell do you think you were conceived? Actually, I think I got pregnant with you while your Faðir had me chained down to the bed," she said nonchalantly while Calder looked absolutely mortified.

I couldn't help but find some amusement in it all, despite the situation, and for that I was glad. This wild group seemed to naturally have this joking, calming effect that helped to turn down the tone when things started to turn stressful, and I think that was one of my favorite things about them all, thus far. It was good to throw in some good to try and ease your thoughts off the bad.

"Okay, enough with traumatizing our sonur," Odin chuckled before turning serious as he looked at me. "Darby, you don't have to leave. As everyone has already said, we can handle it so stop worrying. You are now a part of this family regardless, so don't worry about it," Odin attempted to reassure me.(son)

"Are you sure, Mr. Havard? I really don't want to cause you all any problems," I said, feeling the weight of the guilt that rested on my shoulders heavily.

"First off, you won't be causing any problems in the slightest because we all want you here, and secondly, call me Odin or Faðir since I have a feeling that you'll be sticking around for a very long time," Odin said, making me blush slightly as I nodded. I chanced a glance up to Calder who was already staring down at me with a smile.

"Thank you for, well, everything. Especially for allowing me to stay here with you all," I said, turning back around to look at everyone in the room. I truly was thankful to each and every one of them.

"Don't be ridiculous, hun, it's plain to see how much you and Calder love each other," Sonya said.

Almost immediately at her words, both Calder and I tensed. I moved out of his grip, slowly walking back and away from everyone as my heart began to pound rapidly in my chest, almost painfully so.

"If you'll all excuse me, I want to go take a breather outside," I said hurriedly, not waiting for a response from anyone before I turned and exited the house through a side door off of the kitchen that led to a back patio. I just needed some fresh air to try and calm myself down.

When I stepped outside, I looked around the patio, noting the two arches, one small and one large, on the patio that both overlooked and led out into the backyard from under the covered area. There were four outdoor loveseat sets that were arranged to make it look like outdoor seating for a restaurant, with a glass and wicker coffee table between each set of two love seats that were placed across from each other. There were also two outdoor, chandelier-esque light fixtures that lit up the back patio and ceiling fans to cool it all down for when the heat outside was particularly brutal.

I walked over to the two arches and leaned against one of them, looking out at the backyard. I didn't know what was causing me to panic so much at first, but after a moment, I realized that it was because of Sonya's words. They had affected me in an unexpected way as I came to a sudden realization.

I realized that I loved Calder Havard, and I couldn't deny just how much I truly did after only being with him for such a short time. My fear was that things were moving much too fast and that what I felt for him was significantly stronger than what he felt for me. Being at this point in our newly formed relationship would surely break it before we could get in too deep.

Perhaps we truly were doomed from the start.

A Nerve-Wracking Confession

Calder's POV -

My mom's words shocked the fuck out of me since I hadn't expected her to say anything of that sort. But her words were like a bucket of freezing cold water that was dumped over the top of my head. They were words that I'm almost certain- no, that I AM certain that signify what I feel for Darby.

Love.

I love a man.

Not just any man, MY man.

MY prison guard.

MY Darby Kelby.

Shit, I love Darby and I don't know whether or not he feels the same for me after he panicked and left to get some air. I can't blame him for panicking, hell, I did at first, too. I'm still kind of panicking over this new realization, but I am also happy too. I LOVE DARBY!

"Calder, stop standing here like a stupid, dumb fuck and go out there and tell your guy how you feel about him!" My Faðir said, his words shocking me out of my own head.

"How did you-"

"How did I know that you love Darby?" He asked, and all I could manage was a dumb nod. "It's obvious in the way that you look at him, hold him, and touch him. It's so damn obvious," he chuckled as he wrapped an arm around my Mamma.

"It's just the way that you act around him and the way that he acts around you. It is clear to anyone how deeply you care and feel about one another," my Mamma said simply.

"Maybe so, but there is no fucking possible way that he feels the same for me in the way that I feel for him. I mean, come on, we only just officially started dating yesterday on the plane ride here. It's too soon for me to tell him that I love him!" I fretted, petrified that we were moving too fast. Or that at least I was. This was guaranteed to send him running!

"Honestly, it's really not," Gunnar said, and I frowned as I looked at him in confusion.

"What do you mean?! Of course, it is!" I said.

"Gunnar's right. It's not too early to have fallen in love with him. There is no set time in a relationship for when to tell your significant other that you love them. You tell them you love them when the time is right. And I would say, for you two, that the time is perfect," Bo said, making us all look at him in shock while he just looked confused as he took in all of our shocked faces. "What? What's wrong? What did I do?"

"When the fuck did you get wise and turn into a damn poet with your words?!" Sven exclaimed, all of us agreeing with his statement. In response, Bo gave a shrug as his cheeks flooded with color.

"I don't know. Just saying that kind of felt, I don't know, right, I guess," he stuttered out, sounding shy for the first time in his entire life. I shook my head, chuckling at him but I was still in disbelief by his sudden wisdom. I knew that he was right. I'm not sure why or how, I just did.

"Well, regardless, I need to go find Darby," I said as I walked off, heading to the back door he had exited out of not too long ago, ignoring whatever else the others were saying behind me. That wasn't important right now. Finding Darby and confessing my feelings to him is.

I opened the door, walked out onto the patio, and looked around for a moment before my eyes quickly locked on Darby. He was leaning against one of the patio arches columns, looking out into the backyard, seemingly deep in thought. There was nothing for him to truly be watching or looking at since all there was back here was a large expanse of lush green grass with some shrubs, trees, and other plants on the outskirts that acted as a privacy shield from any potential nosy, onlookers.

I cautiously and quietly walked up behind him, slowly wrapping my arms around his waist, not wanting to frighten him out of whatever he was thinking about. He momentarily tensed up but relaxed shortly after I dropped my head to press a gentle kiss to the side of his neck.

"Hey," he said softly, leaning back into my body more, relaxing against my chest while never taking his eyes off of the backyard.

"You okay?" I said in the same soft tone, earning a sigh from him.

"Yeah. I'm sorry for running off like that. I was just kind of shocked by what your mom said," he apologized.

"Hey, there's no need to apologize, elskan. I was surprised by her words, too, so I understand why you reacted the way that you did," I assured him.

"I should have...well, I'm not sure what I should have done. But running away wasn't the answer, though," he said with a chuckle.

"No, probably not, but I'm just glad you didn't leave," I sighed.

He turned his head to look back at me with a smirk on his lips, one of his eyebrows raised in question.

"Why? Afraid that if I run you'll never be able to find me again?" He teased, earning a scoff from me at his words as I held him closer and tighter to me.

"Funny, elskan. You know that saying 'you can run, but you can't hide'?" I asked, and now it was his turn to scoff.

"Oh, so you think that you'll be able to find me wherever I would go if I were to leave you?" He asked, obviously not believing me and my abilities...or my determination when it came to all things concerning him.

"Oh, I know I would be able to," I said confidently, making him laugh lightly with a small shake of his head.

"Whatever," he conceded.

I smirked as I decided to mess with him some more, knowing that what I had planned on saying would set his cheeks aflame almost instantly.

"Besides, if I told you I'd fuck you, you'd come running back to me since you're pretty desperate for my dick."

He gasped as he turned quickly in my arms, punching me in the shoulder and burying his burning red face in my chest while I tossed my head back, laughing loudly. God, he was so gorgeous when he blushed. And sexy too.

"You're such a fucking asshole," he grumbled against my chest while I continued to laugh, much quieter now. I slowly ran my hand up and down his spine as I smiled down at him, taking note of how fucking adorable he currently looked. His blushing cheeks were hidden from my view and his hands were fisting my shirt, making him almost look like a little kid in my arms from our vast size differences.

"Maybe so, but especially for you," I teased back at him.

"I don't think I'll ever be able to understand why, either," he mumbled into my chest, though I heard him clearly.

"If you really want to know, all you have to do is ask," I said, my tone quickly shifting from playful to serious in a split second. I knew that now was the time to share my feelings for him. To tell him that I loved him.

At the change of my tone, he pulled his head back from my chest and looked at me, curiosity shining brightly in his eyes.

"Why? Why are you such a fucking asshole, especially to me?" He asked softly, looking up at me with his eyes quickly flicking down to my lips before moving back up to my eyes.

"Because Darby...I love you."

Now it's time for the moment of truth. Is he going to say it back to me? Or is he going to tell me that he doesn't feel the same?

Fuck, I've never been so damn nervous in my entire life, and his silence isn't helping!

Worth the Worries

- -

Darby's POV -

When Calder told me to ask him why he was always such a fucking asshole, I had expected something stupid. Like for him to say somewhere along the lines of 'because I'm always horny and want to fuck the shit out of you'.

But no, I didn't get either of those responses from him. Instead, the response I got was:

"Because Darby...I love you."

I stood stock still, just staring up at him for a moment with my eyes slightly wide and my mouth parted just a little in shock. Never in a million fucking years would I have expected to hear those words fall from his lips, especially after having only just discovered that I loved him myself.

"Elskan, please. Say something. Please," he said, practically begging me as he looked down at me with slight panic in his eyes that were otherwise filled with love.

Love for me.

Love that I shared with him.

Without saying a single word, I stood on my tiptoes, leaning up to him and pressing our lips together. I moved my hands up to tangle in the hair at the nape of his neck, lightly tugging at the soft, short strands making him grunt into my open mouth as I slipped my tongue inside his. I wrapped it around his tongue, pulling it back into my mouth where I sucked on the tip of his tongue, causing groans to sound out from the both of us. We kissed slowly for a minute more before Calder pulled back, breaking our slow, passionate kiss as he looked down at me.

"What's wrong?" I asked through soft pants.

"As much as I was enjoying that kiss, I'm not sure whether that was a 'goodbye' kiss or an 'I love you too' kiss," he said.

I couldn't help the soft laugh that escaped my lips as I leaned forward, giving his lips a soft peck and smiling up at him.

"It was definitely an I love you too kiss, Calder," I elaborated for him.

The smile that covered his lips was so big that I was afraid that his face might crack in two. But I couldn't really say much as I wore a smile that matched his.

His hands immediately dropped down to grip my ass before he quickly picked me up, allowing my legs to wrap around his hips. I kept my arms locked around his neck and tangled in his hair, watching as he leaned forward and reconnected our lips for another slow, passionate kiss that had me whining and whimpering for more after we had separated.

"Fuck, I love you," he sighed as he grinned widely at me.

"I love you too," I replied with an equally large grin back at him.

Cheers and applause sounded out from behind Calder's back, prompting him to turn to the side so that we both could see what was going on.

There behind us, all crowded in and around the doorway that came from inside leading to out here, stood everyone: Bo, Gunnar, Odin, Sonya, and Sven. They were all grinning and giving us looks of pure elation.

"I have a feeling that I know the answer to this, but I'm going to ask it anyway: How long have you all been standing there?" Calder asked them with a playful resigned sigh. I could tell that he didn't really mind that they had probably seen and overheard us.

"Long enough to hear you two profess your love, and maybe see you two make out a little," Sonya said bluntly, giggling happily whilst I blushed, burrowing my face into Calder's broad chest. How they were all so direct without a care in the world blew my mind every single time, but I secretly enjoyed the close bond that they all shared.

"You're such a fucking creeper, Mamma!" Calder said with a chuckle, stopping when a phone started to ring. Odin reached into one of his pants pockets, pulled it out, and looked down at the screen for a moment with a slightly furrowed brow.

Odin apologized briefly before stepping back into the house to take the call while we all relaxed out back. We talked happily about Calder and I's relationship until Odin walked back out, sitting next to his wife on one of the loveseats, drawing all of our attention to him as we gave him curious looks at his perplexed look.

"Who called?" Gunnar asked.

"GoldenEye. He said he'll be here tomorrow afternoon," Odin said briefly.

"GoldenEye? What for?" Calder asked.

"He needs some information on someone. A location, specifically, and asked for our help in tracking the person down," Odin replied to which Calder shrugged back.

"Alright. Easy enough."

GoldenEye? Must be a code name for someone. Either way, I don't plan on finding out who they are since it isn't any business of mine. Besides, I was hoping to get out of the house tomorrow and go buy a few shirts and shorts since it's hot as fuck out here and I didn't pack enough for an extended stay like I would be having. Before I hadn't been too happy about that, but now that things with Calder and I have progressed, positively, I know that I'll be just fine here with him for however long. Perhaps even forever.

I turned to look at Calder to tell him my request to see him turning to look back at me with a smile on his face as he leaned in and kissed me gently. Well, it started off gently before he pulled me closer and the kiss grew hungrier as our tongues wrestled and wrapped around one another.

I let out a quiet laugh as I tried to separate our lips only for Calder's to follow mine, not letting my lips get too far away from his. I pushed at his chest to get him to back off, but that proved useless when he just smirked while continuing to kiss me.

"Fucking hell, Calder! Back up for a minute! I wanted to talk to you!" I said, grinning against his lips as he planted them more firmly against mine than before.

"Kiss now. Talk later," he hummed happily against my lips, making me groan at how obnoxiously cute he was being.

I let my hand trail down from his chest to his prominent bulge, wrapping my hand around him the best I could through his pants. I gave him a firm squeeze that made him release a strangled, desperate cry for more.

"No, talk now. Kiss later," I said, successfully pulling away from him.

"Fine, but now that you've touched him, he's going to need special treatment later," he said, nodding down to his dick that was still in my hand making me grin.

"Fine. But now I want to talk to you about tomorrow," I began, easily capturing his full attention.

"Okay, what about it?"

"I'm in need of some more clothes, so I'm going to go shopping tomorrow."

"Alright, that's fine. I'll give you my card tonight so that you can buy what you need. Oh, and you're taking someone else with you," he said instantly, making me scowl.

"I'm fine with taking someone else with me, but I'm not using your card," I denied.

"Yes, you are. If you want to buy something, you buy it with my card. If I find out you didn't use my card on something or you just didn't use it at all, I'm chaining your ass to our bed and I'm fucking you so damn hard that you won't be able to sit down or walk properly for days," he threatened. Honestly, that punishment didn't sound half bad. I might do it on purpose just to force his hand.

I patted his cheek gently as I stood up, finally releasing his bulge.

"You better find those chains, Viking man of mine, because I'm going to need that punishment," I said, turning to walk inside as I noticed everyone else doing the same seeing as it was time to get some dinner. Time seemed to just fly by today, it was insane how fast the day had gone by. It probably had something to do with all of today's events and activities.

With a growl, Calder stood as well, quickly scooping me up into his arms as he carried me inside.

"Something tells me that you won't find that to be much of a punishment," he said quietly as he nipped at my ear, a wide smirk appearing on my face as I looked at him.

"Probably because I won't."

He groaned as I laughed at his dramatics.

God how I love teasing him. Almost as much as I love him.

Flustered

The next morning, I woke up curled into Calder's chest with his arms wrapped around me tightly. Our bodies, naked from the previous night, were pressed as close as we could get to one another.

I looked up to see Calder's eyes were shut, his lashes resting against his upper cheeks with his mouth opened just a touch as small puffs of air were let out on each breath. Even as I looked at him and how he appeared to be sleeping, I could tell that he was awake by the way his mouth was set in a way that showed he was attempting to conceal a smirk.

I moved my hand, which was placed atop his right pectoral, down his side, sliding it slowly over his hip. I moved lower, down to his thick, hard shaft that was pressed against my thigh, beginning to stroke it slowly as I leaned up to kiss his jaw before slowly kissing my way over to his ear, gently sucking on his ear lobe before giving it a nip.

"Mmm," he moaned into my ear, making my smirk grow wider.

"I knew you were awake," I said quietly, continuing to gently suck his ear lobe into my mouth.

"Mmm, and if I wasn't?" He grunted, both of his hands moving down to squeeze my sore ass, resulting in me moaning despite my aching.

"I have a feeling that you wouldn't have minded this wake-up call," I said, trailing kisses down his jaw, shifting my body so I was now lying atop him. My hand continued stroking his shaft as his hands remained firmly planted on my ass.

"Oh, I definitely wouldn't have minded," he grunted as I began to move my kisses down his chest, slowly moving even further down his body.

"What do you say to me making your morning even better?" I hummed out against his solid abs.

"Oh yeah?" He said back huskily.

"Mhm."

"What did you have in mind?" He asked, watching me closely. His hands fell from my ass as I settled down between his spread legs, peering up at him with a smirk.

"Maybe...this," I said, ceasing my stroking as I leaned forward and replaced my hand with my mouth, locking it around the head of his cock.

I sucked on him hard, running the tip of my tongue teasingly over his slit, collecting the precum that had leaked out and moaning at the taste. I kept my eyes trained on him the entire time, watching the intense look of pleasure that crossed his features as his eyes trailed every one of my motions.

"Oh, fuck, elskan! Mmm!" He moaned as he bucked his hips up, sending his cock deeper down my throat which I happily accepted. I sucked more on his shaft before beginning to bob my head, paying the rest of his cock attention instead of just his sensitive tip. I started out slowly before gradually picking up my pace, sucking harder as I let my tongue wrap around his shaft while moving my head and mouth up and down his length.

"FUCK! GAHHH!" He cried out, pushing my head down further so that the head of his cock was now hitting the back of my throat. I let out a contented hum at the feeling and at the sight of him writhing at my mercy.

I moved my head up and down two more times, letting the head hit the back of my throat each time. When I went to do it for a third time, he let out a loud moan as he released his seed straight down my throat which I greedily gulped down.

Once he'd finished cumming, I pulled my mouth off of his dick, giving the head of his cock a final swipe with my tongue before moving back up to the top of the bed, alongside him. I relaxed on my side next to him, watching as he panted heavily with his eyes closed and his head thrown back on his pillows.

"Did I do okay? I've never done that before and I wanted to try it, but I-" I said, starting to ramble but Calder clamped his hand across my mouth, effectively silencing my nervous and worried words as he looked at me with a wide, toothy grin.

"Elskan shut up. I think you know damn good and well how much I enjoyed every fucking second of that blowjob," he said with a chuckle, removing his hand to see my delighted smile.

"Good. You should be thankful that I don't have a gag reflex so that I was able to deepthroat you like that. Because I promise you that if I did, I wouldn't have let you try and gag me with your cock," I said as he wrapped his arm around me to pull me closer to him.

"Oh, don't worry. I am very glad for your lack of a gag reflex," he said, leaning down to peck my lips a few times before we both got out of bed. We headed to the bathroom where we showered and brushed our teeth before getting dressed and heading down to the kitchen.

Calder wore another red outfit that was similar to the one he wore the day prior. It consisted of another red long-sleeved shirt though this one was a button-up and was stretched taut against his broad, muscled form that looked seconds away from shredding it. He also wore another pair of black ripped jeans, but instead of just the knees being ripped like the others, the rips in these began at his mid-thighs and then proceeded down his legs, though not excessively, and he wore black ankle socks with red high-top sneakers. I, on the other hand, wore a short-sleeved sky-blue floral shirt with white, light red, and yellow hibiscus', a pair of dark grey jeans, and white socks and sneakers.

Once we reached the kitchen, I noted that everyone else in the house was already there, scattered between the kitchen and the attached sitting area.

"Damn, look at you, Darby!" Gunnar whistled.

"Who are you trying to impress?" Bo asked as he and Gunnar snickered at each other while I rolled my eyes at them and their stupidity.

"Not a damn soul. My clothing choices are limited so I have to work with what I've got for now, but I'm going shopping after breakfast," I explained.

"Who's going with you?" Calder asked, and I turned to look at Sven and Sonya.

"Sven, Sonya, I was wondering if you guys would go with me?" I said, even though it sounded more like an uncertain question.

"Sure, I'm fine with that," Sven shrugged.

"Yes! I can't wait!" Sonya squealed excitedly, clapping her hands together excitedly.

"For fucks sake, Darby, why would you invite her? She's already got more shit than she knows what to do with!" Odin groaned, resting his head on the countertop.

Sonya, who was cooking something in a frying pan on the stove, turned to Odin and smacked him on his ass with the spatula she held in her hand. He shot up, letting out a shocked cry as she glared at him.

"Stop being a jerk! You've never had a problem before!" She shrieked at him.

"Sonya, I love you to death, but you buy so much useless shit," Odin replied.

She crossed her arms over her chest, suddenly smirking at him with an angry glint in her eyes.

"Well then, you better prepare for even more 'useless shit', as you call it, once we come home," she said.

Calder chuckled as he wrapped his arms around me, pulling me closer to him as he pressed a kiss to the top of my head.

"Ha, you're fucked, Faðir! I can't even barely get Darby to use my card and then you went and pissed off Mamma so now she's going to try and max out yours!" Calder mocked Odin. I rolled my eyes at Calder as I pulled out of his grip and walked into the dining room where we were going to be eating breakfast in just a matter of minutes. Calder followed right behind me, sitting down next to me once I had chosen a seat, tossing his arm over my shoulder and pulling me back into his side.

"Why the hell are you following Darby like you're a dog, Calder?" Gunnar chuckled.

"Because I love him and I can," he shot back.

"Or could it have something to do with whatever happened in your bedroom this morning?" Bo asked.

Almost instantly Calder was breaking out into a massive, cocky grin as he looked down at me as my face went red. I already had a pretty good idea of where this was about to be headed.

"Oh, this morning was fucking AMAZING! The best morning of my life!" He exclaimed excitedly as his parents and Sven walked in carrying breakfast plates for all of us.

"Why was this morning the best morning of your life?" Odin asked, and I quickly whirled on Calder.

"Don't you fucking dare say a word!" I threatened, but he, of course, didn't listen and replied anyway.

"My elskan here gave me the best fucking blowjob of my life!"

I buried my face in my hands, blushing as I shook my head back and forth.

"Calder! No sexual talk at the table!" Sonya scolded him.

"Sorry, Mamma!" He said, not sounding the least bit apologetic. I shook my head again as I began to eat, still embarrassed by Calder and his bluntness, but I wouldn't have him any other way.

We ate, all of us happy and content, before beginning to separate once we had all finished up. I headed upstairs to grab my phone from the nightstand, having left Calder downstairs to talk business with Odin since he would be retaking his position as the head again, now that he was no longer in the Penitentiary. After I picked up my phone, I turned it on and quickly swiped away all of the missed calls and texts from my Dad, hoping that he wasn't currently trying to track my location. I faintly heard the sound of the doorbell ringing as I made my way back to the stairs, figuring that it was probably that GoldenEye person.

Once I reached the stairs, I descended them quickly as I followed the sound of Odin and Calder's voices. I wanted to tell Calder that I was going to head out once Sonya came downstairs and I figured out wherever the hell Sven had wandered off to since I knew that Calder would flip out if he needed me for something while I was out and I didn't answer him, he would instantly start thinking about the worst possible thing that could have happened to me.

I walked through the house, heading straight to the sitting area closest to Calder's office where I saw both Odin and Calder standing there facing me. There was also a man, who I presumed to be GoldenEye, who was standing in front of them with his back to me, but I just ignored him as I headed straight to Calder.

"Elskan, you heading out now?" Calder smiled at me as he saw me coming in.

"Yeah, once your mom gets downstairs and I locate Sven," I replied.

"Alright, come get my card and I want a kiss before you go," he said.

I rolled my eyes at him with a small smile on my lips. My cheeks flushed a soft pink at the fact that some guy I didn't know was going to see Calder and I kiss. But I walked over to Calder anyway as he pulled out his card and handed it to me. I slipped it into the back pocket of my jeans and leaned forward, pressing a quick peck to Calder's lips.

"This is Calder's boyfriend, he's a great guy. His name is-" Odin began to introduce me to this GoldenEye guy, only to be cut off.

"Darby?!"